The Farnsworth Invention

by Aaron Sorkin

A SAMUEL FRENCH ACTING EDITION

SAMUEL FRENCH

FOUNDED 1830

NEW YORK HOLLYWOOD LONDON TORONTO

SAMUELFRENCH.COM

ISBN 978-0-573-66286-7   Printed in U.S.A.   #8213

IMPORTANT BILLING AND CREDIT REQUIREMENTS

All producers of *THE FARNSWORTH INVENTION must* give credit to the Author of the Play in all programs distributed in connection with performances of the Play, and in all instances in which the title of the Play appears for the purposes of advertising, publicizing or otherwise exploiting the Play and/or a production. The name of the Author *must* appear on a separate line on which no other name appears, immediately following the title and *must* appear in size of type not less than fifty percent of the size of the title type.

In addition the following credit *must* be given in all programs and publicity information distributed in association with this piece:

"A Page to Stage Production of The Farnsworth Invention
Produced in 2007 by The La Jolla Playhouse, La Jolla, California
Christopher Ashley, Artistic Director & Steven Libman,
Managing Director"

"Original Broadway Production by Produced by Dodger Properties, Steven Spielberg and Rabbit Ears, LLC; Produced in association with Frederick Zollo, Jeffrey Sine, Dancap Productions, Inc., Latitude Link and Pelican Group; Associate Producer: Lauren Mitchell"

THE FARNSWORTH INVENTION opened on Dec 3, 2007 at The Music Box Theater in New York City, produced by Dodger Properties, Steven Spielberg and Rabbit Ears, LLC; in association with Frederick Zollo, Jeffrey Sine, Dancap Productions, Inc., Latitude Link and Pelican Group. The Associate Producer was Lauren Mitchell, Executive Producer was Sally Campbell Morse. The production was directed by Des McAnuff with the following cast and creative staff:

DAVID SARNOFF . . . . Hank Azaria
LIZETTE SARNOFF, MARY PICKFORD and others . . . . Nadia Bowers
PEM'S FATHER, CLIFF GARDNER and others . . . . Kyle Fabel
ATKINS, WALTER GIFFORD,
DOUGLAS FAIRBANKS and others . . . . Maurice Godin
YOUNG PHILO T. FARNSWORTH and others . . . Christian M. Johansen
WILKINS, ANALYST and others . . . . Aaron Krohn
GEORGE EVERSON,
VLADIMIR ZWORYKIN and others . . . . Bruce Mckenzie
YOUNG DAVID SARNOFF and others . . . . Malcolm Morano
STAN WILLIS and others . . . . Spencer Moses
LESLIE GORRELL and others . . . . Michael Mulheren
JUSTIN TOLMAN,
JIM HARBORD, DOCTOR and others . . . . Jim Ortlieb
SARNOFF'S FATHER, SIMMS, LIPPINCOTT,
HOUSTON CONTROL and others . . . . Michael Pemberton
BETTY AND OTHERS . . . . Katharine Powell
HARLAN HONN,
RADIO ANNOUNCER,LENNOX and others . . . . Steve Rosen
PHILO T. FARNSWORTH . . . . Jimmi Simpson
RUSSIAN OFFICER, WILLIAM CROCKER and others . . . James Sutorius
SARNOFF'S MOTHER, PEM'S MOTHER,
AGNES FARNSWORTH, MINA EDISON and others . . . . . Margot White
PEM FARNSWORTH and others . . . . Alexandra Wilson
WACHTEL and others . . . . William Youmans

Assistant Director: Daisy Walker
Scenic Design: Klara Zieglerova
Costume Design: David C. Woolard
Lighting Design: Howell Binkley
Sound Design: Walter Trarbach
Hair and Wig Design: Mark Adam Rampmeyer
Company Manager: Jennifer Hindman Kemp
General Manager: Dodger Management Group
Production Stage Manager: Frank Hartenstein
Technical Supervisor: Peter Fulbright and Tech Production Services, Inc.
Stage Manager: Kelly Martindale
Assistant Stage Manager: Stephanie Atlan

ACT I

(Aa the audience enters, a scrim curtain is down. The curtain is a huge diagram of Philo Farnsworth's television operating system, complete with indecipherable equations and ungodly electronic components.)

(The scrim conceals the playing area, a raked stage which will have to serve many purposes. The action should flow from scene to scene seamlessly, with a new scene being defined by a sudden lighting change, a sound cue or a set piece being slammed.)

(With the exception of the principals, actors will double and triple in roles.)

(As the house lights go out, a small pool of light comes up behind the scrim revealing **DAVID SARNOFF.***)*

(SARNOFF *is of indeterminate age but he's an alpha male. Confident with a dry wit, he's generally the smartest person in any room he walks into. He doesn't suffer fools but he's able to recognize character and intelligence in his enemies, of which he has many.)*

(He addresses the audience directly and informally.)

SARNOFF. Good evening, I'm David Sarnoff. There's a rule in storytelling that says you never tell your audience something they already know but I'm gonna chance it anyway by starting like this: the only reason you can see me right now is because light is reflecting off of me. *Light* bounces and I wanted to make sure everyone knew that or 20 minutes in you're gonna be thinking what in the hell is happening? Can we show everyone else?

(Pools of light hit up on the other **ACTORS** *in the cast placed variously around the stage.)*

SARNOFF. *(continued)* Thank you.

(The CAST *exits.)*

You also need to know that 17 is a very important number but I'm gonna remind of you of that later. And by the way the ends do justify the means, *that's what means are for.* Now it's 1921 and not a lot of people were thinking about electrons except the writers of comic books and the readers of comic books, one of whom was a kid from Indian Creek, Utah whose family had just moved to Rigby, Idaho to live on his uncle's potato farm. If there are any Brits in the house they're gonna start shouting John Logie Baird at me but they're wrong, Baird didn't have it. Neither did Nipkow or Ernst Alexanderson and neither did Vladimir Zworykin. I know they didn't have it 'cause I knew these men and Zworykin worked for me. Nobody had it, nobody was close and lemme tell you nobody cared that much 'cause at best it was gonna be considered a nifty parlor trick. Nobody had it except a 14-year-old kid in Rigby, Idaho standing in a field of potatoes. He rode a three-disc plow, drawn by a mule, making three parallel lines in the earth at once. Then three more. Then three more and three more until he was done with his work. He stepped off the plow, looked back at the rows and rows of parallel lines, and that's when he realized the key to the most influential invention in history. So he did what any world-class electrical engineer would do in that situation: He went to see his 9th grade science teacher.

(LIGHTS CHANGE TO:)

Classroom

(Where **TOLMAN** *is working at his desk.* **YOUNG PHILO** *taps on the open door.)*

YOUNG PHILO. Excuse me.

TOLMAN. Yeah.

YOUNG PHILO. Mr. Tolman?

TOLMAN. What can I do for you?

YOUNG PHILO. Are you Mr. Tolman?

TOLMAN. Yeah.

YOUNG PHILO. My name's Philo Farnsworth. My family just moved here, I'm starting school on Monday.

TOLMAN. Well you're gonna have me for Basic Science.

YOUNG PHILO. I wanted to ask you about that.

TOLMAN. Yeah.

YOUNG PHILO. I was wondering if I could skip Basic Science and take your chemistry class instead.

TOLMAN. You've gotta have Basic Science before you can take Chemistry.

YOUNG PHILO. I understand.

TOLMAN. Good.

YOUNG PHILO. I think that's perfectly reasonable.

TOLMAN. Thanks. *(pause)* Anything else?

YOUNG PHILO. Could I ask you a quick question?

SARNOFF. *(to the audience)* Remember, it's 1921, the guy hasn't started ninth grade and we're in Huckleberry, Idaho. Listen to what comes out of his mouth.

YOUNG PHILO. When light hits photoelectric material it releases a spray of electrons, right?

TOLMAN. Hm?

SARNOFF. "Hm?" This is Justin Tolman, by the way. He's a decent enough guy but he'll be easy to destroy during depositions. Right now he has no idea what's just walked into his classroom. Go ahead, ask the question again.

YOUNG PHILO. Photoelectric material, like, say, selenium, it releases a spray of electrons when light hits it?

TOLMAN. Yeah.

YOUNG PHILO. And a cathode does essentially the opposite, right? It takes invisible electrons and makes them glow?

TOLMAN. *(beat)* I think so.

YOUNG PHILO. Okay. Thank you.

(And **PHILO** *exits –)*

TOLMAN. What the hell –

SARNOFF. Yeah, get used to it, my friend.

(to the audience)

He'd already told his father about the idea. He'd explained that "tele" was Greek. It meant "distant." Vision from a distance. Television. The father said he shouldn't repeat this stuff to anyone else 'cause no one would take him seriously again. This is like Toscanini's dad telling him no one's gonna take you seriously with that stick in your hand. *(beat)* It's Tuesday, second day of school.

(A school bell rings –)

TOLMAN. *(to the class)* All right, that's it. Everyone put the homework assignments on my desk as you leave this room as quickly and quietly as possible.

(The students are filing out, dropping off the homework on the desk –)

SARNOFF. It was a one-page assignment from the front of the textbook.

TOLMAN. Whoa, whoa, what's this?

YOUNG PHILO. Homework.

TOLMAN. This is last night's homework?

YOUNG PHILO. No, I just went ahead and did it for the whole year, is that okay?

*(***TOLMAN*** starts leafing through* **PHILO**'*s pages.)*

TOLMAN. All right, you know what, you stay for a second. The rest of you, let's go. C'mon, let's go.

(The rest of the students exit…)

TOLMAN. Kid. Your father, he works for the government? He's a scientist?

YOUNG PHILO. He's a potato farmer.

TOLMAN. You read at home?

YOUNG PHILO. Yes sir.

TOLMAN. Tesla?

YOUNG PHILO. Yes.

TOLMAN. Edison?

YOUNG PHILO. Yeah.

TOLMAN. Marconi?

YOUNG PHILO. Yes.

TOLMAN. What else?

YOUNG PHILO. I like the Sears Roebuck catalogue.

TOLMAN. Okay, well, you've passed Basic Science.

YOUNG PHILO. Hey thanks, that's great news.

*(And **PHILO** just stands there…)*

TOLMAN. *(pause)* That's it.

YOUNG PHILO. Can I draw something for you?

TOLMAN. Excuse me?

YOUNG PHILO. Can I draw something for you?

TOLMAN. Yeah.

*(**TOLMAN** hands him a piece of paper and **PHILO** starts drawing –)*

YOUNG PHILO. *(while he's drawing)* You trap light in an empty jar, roughly the size of what your mother would use to keep fruit fresh only it would have to be a vacuum jar. A vacuum jar, and the inside of the jar is treated with a special surface that reacts to light and converts it into electrical impulses. And we scan the impulses. Line by line. 50, 60 lines, I don't know, 500 lines. The effect would be instantaneous but in actuality we'd be reading it line by line. The way we plow a field.

TOLMAN. Son, the cathode, the selenium, the vacuum jar, what's all this about?

YOUNG PHILO & PHILO. I think there's a way to transmit pictures electronically through the air the way we're doing with sound and radio.

(And this last line was spoken by the adult **PHILO FARN-SWORTH** *who's walked up behind his childhood self to deliver the punchline to the scene.)*

*(***PHILO***'s a few years younger than* **SARNOFF**. *He has a quick, often self-deprecating wit, and like a giant who's careful not to trample a mouse,* **PHILO** *knows not to use his intellect to pick on anyone who isn't his own size.* **SAR-NOFF**'*s the only man who's ever met that description.)*

(As soon as **PHILO** *says the word "radio," it begins to rain and a* **RUSSIAN POLICE OFFICER** *enters shouting –)*

RUSSIAN OFFICER. *Komendah! Zazhgite fakuly!*

(LIGHTS CHANGE TO:)

Uzlian Shtetl

(As some more **OFFICERS** *enter with lit torches.)*

PHILO. *(to the audience)* Shtetl is a Yiddish word that means ghetto and this shtetl was in the Uzlian Province of, I think, Minsk, but I'm not sure, there's a lot about his history that's a little cloudy to me.

OFFICER. *Komendah!*

(Upstage, a little **BOY** *and his* **PARENTS** *are packing the last of their stuff onto a wagon —)*

PHILO. Sarnoff's 10-years-old when the Czar sends the cops to empty out the village.

OFFICER. *Zazhgite fakuly!*

PHILO. *(to* **SARNOFF***)* Translate the Russian please.

SARNOFF. I don't remember a lot of Russian.

PHILO. You remember this.

SARNOFF. It had something to do with lighting the —

PHILO. Translate the damn Russian.

SARNOFF. *(beat)* Komendah means — it's "company," "battalion," he's calling to the other officers.

PHILO. Zazhgite fakuly?

SARNOFF. Light the torches.

PHILO. An officer comes up to the boy.

OFFICER. *(in Russian — to the* **BOY***)* Ne nada bayat'sia. My ne zveri.

SARNOFF. *(translating)* Don't be scared, we're not monsters.

OFFICER. *(in Russian)* U tvaego atsa mnoga knig.

SARNOFF. *(translating)* Your father has a lot of books.

OFFICER. *(in Russian)* Ty lyubish knigi?

SARNOFF. *(translating)* Do you like books?

PHILO. And 10-year-old Sarnoff says to the armed Russian officer… ?

YOUNG SARNOFF. *(in Russian)* Pashol k chortu.

SARNOFF. Go fuck yourself.

OFFICER. *(pause – in Russian) Chto ty skazal?*

SARNOFF. What did you say?

YOUNG SARNOFF. *(in Russian) Nichevo.*

SARNOFF. I didn't say anything.

OFFICER. *(in Russian) Ladna.*

SARNOFF. Good.

YOUNG SARNOFF. *(in Russian) Tol'ko pashel by ty k chortu.*

SARNOFF. *(translating)* Except go fuck yourself.

OFFICER. *(in Russian) Paslushai, druzhischa.*

SARNOFF. Take your hand off me before I make you shoot me in front of 200 people.

YOUNG SARNOFF. Uberi ruki, a to budesh vynuzhden zastrelit' menya pri vsekh.

PHILO. And then they burned his house down while he watched. The family moved to the lower east side of Manhattan where Sarnoff sold Yiddish newspapers on a street corner. His father died when he was 13 and by 14 he had absolutely no trace of a Russian accent. The New York Herald was hiring messenger boys and he went in for the job but when he got to the Herald building he went into the wrong office.

(LIGHTS CHANGE TO:)

Office

(Where **TWO MEN** *are working at a desk and a third is sitting at a table. The* **THIRD MAN** *has headphones on and is transcribing a message at a wireless set.)*

(YOUNG SARNOFF *walks in –)*

MAN #1. Can I help you?

YOUNG SARNOFF. The paper said you need messenger boys and I'd like the job.

MAN #1. This isn't the *Herald*, you're in the wrong office, you want to go down the hall.

YOUNG SARNOFF. I'm sorry?

MAN #1. This isn't the newspaper, we just lease office space here. This is the Commercial Cable Company.

YOUNG SARNOFF. Sorry.

MAN #1. Not a problem, you want to be down the hall.

(And **YOUNG SARNOFF** *starts to leave but stops…)*

YOUNG SARNOFF. What do you do?

MAN #1. We send and receive cable messages. *(beat)* Radio, you heard of it?

PHILO. He was in love. I know how he felt. It took him a week and a half to become the company's best wireless operator but they fired him anyway 'cause he wouldn't work on the Jewish holidays. That was fine, though, 'cause it set the stage for his first triumph and it was on a massive scale.

(LIGHTS CHANGE TO:)

American Marconi

(Something's going on. There's a large crowd and people are being held back by a few police officers.)

(YOUNG SARNOFF is manning a wireless machine. Every once in a while he'll shout out a name to the crowd as he writes it down.)

YOUNG SARNOFF. *(shouting)* James Cooley! James W. Cooley!

PHILO. He'd been hired by American Marconi, the American arm of the British owned Marconi Wireless Telegraph and Signal Company. American Marconi rented a tiny room on the second floor of Wannamaker's Department Store. On this night, the police were handling the crowd that was growing down on the street and there were even a few officers upstairs with some V.I.P.'s that had been let in. It was Sunday night and 30 hours earlier, the *Parisian*, a passenger ship about 300 nautical miles off the coast of Nova Scotia, had gotten a radio message.

YOUNG SARNOFF. *(calling out)* Mrs. William Christiansen.

(WACHTEL makes his way through the crowd at the door and over to SIMMS, who's busy and energized –)

WACHTEL. Eddie, what the hell is going on, I've been on a train from Chicago for sixteen hours –

SIMMS. The *Carpathia's* got 712 survivors on board.

WACHTEL. Confirmed?

SIMMS. Yes.

WACHTEL. How do we know?

SIMMS. They radioed another ship, the *Parisian* and we're on with 'em right now.

WACHTEL. They've got the names?

YOUNG SARNOFF. *(calling out)* Douglas W. Winston.

(SIMMS stops his movement...)

SIMMS. *We've* got the names.

YOUNG SARNOFF. Winslow. I'm sorry, Douglas W. Winslow.

WACHTEL. Are you telling me we're the only ones with the names of the survivors?

SIMMS. Yeah.

WACHTEL. How the hell did – ?

SIMMS. We got all the other wireless stations on the Atlantic coast to shut down to avoid interference.

WACHTEL. Would there have been interference?

SIMMS. No!

WACHTEL. Who got them to do that?

SIMMS. *(indicating* YOUNG SARNOFF *)* He did.

YOUNG SARNOFF. *(shouting out)* Mr. and Mrs. Theodore Meriweather.

WOMAN FROM THE CROWD. And Julianne? Julianne Meri-weather?

*(*YOUNG SARNOFF *holds up his hand to indicate "just a moment" –)*

WACHTEL. Who is that?

SIMMS. He got fired from the Commercial Cable Company 'cause he wouldn't work on Hannukah or something, I don't know what the fuck, but he's been sitting there for 30 hours straight, he won't give up the chair.

WACHTEL. What's his name?

SIMMS. David Sarnoff.

PHILO. And American Marconi was on the map. Or at least on the map enough to catch the attention of the War Department, which decided that it probably wasn't a good idea to have a foreign company install-ing electronic communications systems in our ships. By Congressional mandate, American Marconi had to be sold and they asked the General Electric Corpora-tion to pick it up for some lunch money. GE did their duty and at a press conference held on Sarnoff's 22nd birthday, with Sarnoff and his beautiful French wife, the former Lizette Hermant, Jim Harbord announced that GE had acquired American Marconi and was con-verting its assets into a new company.

CHAIRMAN. *(from the podium)* The Radio Corporation of America.

(And the RCA logo, to much applause, is revealed by **TWO SEXY WOMEN** *on either side of an easel.)*

PHILO. Sarnoff was appointed Commercial Manager at 45 dollars-a-week. It was an executive job but the one no one else wanted. The job meant coming up with new uses for radio, and other than, "Please help me my boat is sinking," there were no other uses for radio and the other guys who'd founded the company with him gave him a hard time about it. In fact, at the press conference, one of two colleagues asked him exactly what did he have in mind for future uses and Sarnoff coolly responded –

SARNOFF. Farm reports.

SIMMS. What?

SARNOFF. Weather reports for farmers.

PHILO. He kind of walked away to listen to the rest of the press conference, so these two guys never heard him add –

SARNOFF. And music.

PHILO. And music is right. Information and entertainment. Why? Because Sarnoff's vision for radio wasn't one person talking to another person, it was one person talking to a million people. A network of radio stations, all under the RCA banner, broadcasting a signal to millions of living rooms with RCA radio receivers.

SARNOFF. He was out of high school, out of the Navy and after a year at Brigham Young, ran out of money for tuition. It was time to build a television set. Through a series of letters, Farnsworth made an appointment to see George Everson and Leslie Gorrell at the local Community Chest in Provo.

(LIGHTS CHANGE TO:)

Community Chest

(Where **EVERSON** *and* **GORRELL** *are sitting and working.)*

SARNOFF. Professionally, Everson and Gorrell were fundraisers for charitable organizations, but privately they'd been considering investing some of their own money in technology, though what they probably had in mind was farm technology.

(And **PHILO** *'s entered the storefront office –)*

EVERSON. I'm George Everson.

PHILO. Philo Farnsworth.

EVERSON. This is my partner, Leslie Gorrell.

GORRELL. Philo's an unusual name.

PHILO. My grandfather was an officer in the Civil War and he got the name from –

GORRELL. Which side?

PHILO. I'm sorry?

GORRELL. Which side was he on in the war?

EVERSON. Leslie.

GORRELL. I'm not allowed to ask which side?

EVERSON. It's not polite.

GORRELL. *It was a war, George!*

EVERSON. He's upset today because our car won't run.

GORRELL. And you gotta tell people?

EVERSON. We went in on a car together.

PHILO. That Chandler roadster outside?

EVERSON. He hates the car. 75 dollars-a-piece. Mint condition, reliable. Comfortable, speeds up to 50 miles –

GORRELL. Reliable?

EVERSON. Excuse me, but that car has been –

GORRELL. The car is sitting in front of the – *it's inert!* What should we rely upon it for exactly?

EVERSON. Maybe if we exhibited a more business-like demeanor and stuck to the matter at hand.

GORRELL. Sure.

EVERSON. Thank you.

GORRELL. *(pause)* What the hell was your name again?

PHILO. Philo Farnsworth.

GORRELL. And what do you want?

PHILO. I need $20,000 to set up a lab and create a device that'll transmit pictures, moving pictures, electronically through the air, and then reassemble them at great distances, all in a fraction of a second.

GORRELL. *(pause)* Hm?

PHILO. You see if you can convert a light image into many horizontal lines –

GORRELL. No, you want how much?

PHILO. $20,000. *(beat)* It's a lot, but it's what I believe it'll take to create a working prototype. Bare bones. You have to understand we'd be starting with nothing but a work-table and a generator so I'd have to –

GORRELL. This is the Community Chest.

PHILO. Yes.

GORRELL. We're fundraisers.

PHILO. Yeah.

GORRELL. We raise money for charities. There's a flood, a town needs a new school, that's what we like.

PHILO. But your letter said you might be interested in investing in a new –

GORRELL. What letter?

EVERSON. I sent him a letter.

PHILO. It was in response to my letter.

GORRELL. Which said?

PHILO. That I was seeking investors for an idea I have for something that would transmit pictures through the air.

GORRELL. *(turning to* EVERSON*)* Are you losing your mind?

PHILO. If it helps, I can tell you that sound would be synchronized and transmitted simultaneously.

GORRELL. Would it?

PHILO. Yes.

GORRELL. *(to* **EVERSON***)* And you wrote back saying?

EVERSON. That it sounded very interesting.

GORRELL. Okay, let's stop here, 'cause –

EVERSON. We always talk about maybe getting involved in an endeavor.

GORRELL. *(to* **PHILO***)* Yeah, what is it you want to do?

PHILO. I want to transmit moving images electronically through the air, capture them again in a cathode ray tube and then project them onto a screen in your house.

*(***GORRELL** *looks at* **EVERSON** *–)*

EVERSON. Why not?

GORRELL. Because I didn't understand a fucking word this kid just said and neither did you.

EVERSON. So let's hear him say more.

GORRELL. Why?

PHILO. 'cause while you're listening I'm gonna fix your car.

SARNOFF. And he did.

(LIGHTS CHANGE TO:)

The Street

(At the Chandler Roadster:)

SARNOFF. *(continued)* I have no reason not to believe his biographers when they say he started the car.

PHILO. Which is probably more than we can say for the Titanic story.

SARNOFF. Excuse me?

PHILO. Wannamaker's has never been open on Sunday.

SARNOFF. Listen you ridiculous hayseed-savant, I'm the world's first communications mogul, you don't think we fucking knew how to get into our – nevermind. There were 712 survivors, you want me to name 'em? Meriweather, Cooley, Dobson, Dotson, Winslow – Phil, there's no reason for me to make this shit up.

PHILO. *(calling to* **EVERSON***)* Keys?

(EVERSON *tosses* **PHILO** *the keys and* **PHILO** *gets under the hood.)*

EVERSON. Your letter said you were in the Navy.

PHILO. Yes sir.

(to **GORRELL***)*

The *U.S.* Navy.

GORRELL. Thank you.

EVERSON. Why'd you leave?

PHILO. Anything you invent while you're in the Navy belongs to the Navy.

EVERSON. So how does it work?

PHILO. It's been demonstrated repeatedly that electrons can be influenced to travel in a beam if they're shot through a vacuum and aimed with a properly shaped magnetic field, did any of that mean anything to either one of you?

GORRELL. No.

EVERSON. Sure.

GORRELL. Shut up.

PHILO. A glass vacuum tube. Now the beam of electrons is aimed at lines of phosphor dots. Magnetic fields of precise shape, strength, and duration.

GORRELL. I understood the words "tube" and "dots."

PHILO. Let's start at the beginning, an electron behaves in the following manner:

GORRELL. You're saying that you can send a photograph from here to there electronically?

(**PHILO** *gets out from under the hood.*)

PHILO. I can but that's not what I'm saying. I'm saying I can send a live moving image from here to there electronically.

GORRELL. Well I wouldn't say it out loud to that many people, but for the sake of amusing myself, how far and how fast?

PHILO. As far as you want and roughly at the speed of light.

(**PHILO** *turns the key and the engine starts.*)

PHILO *(continued)* I also adjusted your carburetor.

(**GORRELL** *looks at* **PHILO** *…then reaches in and turns off the car.*)

GORRELL. We don't have $20,000.

EVERSON. We don't. We don't have $20,000, but we do have $3000 earmarked –

GORRELL. George –

EVERSON. Leslie, for an endeavor.

PHILO. Well, $3000 would –

GORRELL. No.

EVERSON. I say we take him to see Crocker.

GORRELL. No.

EVERSON. Crocker likes science. He loves science. He funded the radiation lab up there where they're doing cancer research.

GORRELL. *(to* **PHILO***)* Your thing, what are you calling it?

PHILO. Television. It's from the Greek word for –

GORRELL. Does it prevent cancer?

PHILO. No.

GORRELL. *(to* **EVERSON***)* Then no.

EVERSON. We're going there anyway. We take him with us and arrange a meeting.

GORRELL. *(to* **PHILO***)* You fixed our car...and you know a lot of big words, most of which I think you're making up, but I'll spring for a train ticket and arrange the meeting.

EVERSON. Great.

GORRELL. And that's it.

PHILO. Where are we going?

SARNOFF. San Francisco to see William Crocker.

(LIGHTS CHANGE TO:)

Meeting Room

SARNOFF. *(continued)* Everson and Gorrell knew Crocker 'cause he was a regional director for Community Chest and he'd made a hobby out of funding scientific research which he could afford to do 'cause he was also the president of Crocker First National Bank. Oh, and his family built the Union-Pacific Railroad.

(**PHILO** *is making his presentation to* **CROCKER** *and a couple of his* **DEPUTIES,** *along with* **EVERSON & GORRELL.** *He stands in front of a large chalk board, filled from edge to edge with various diagrams. It looks like future world. As he speaks, he's animated, like a teacher who loves teaching.)*

SARNOFF. *(continued)* He'd been given strict instructions by Gorrell to keep it short. Try for 15 minutes but no more than 20. He began his presentation at exactly 10 AM and finished it at ten minutes past two.

PHILO. Now, I need lab space, a worktable, a glassblower and a high quality vacuum pump. I'll need to make some precision tools. *(pause)* Any questions?

ATKINS. The signal can only travel in a straight line, right?

PHILO. Yes sir.

ATKINS. How do you account for tall buildings, mountains, or the curvature of the Earth for that matter?

PHILO. I could bounce the signal off a series of stationary balloons.

WILKINS. Who else is working on television?

PHILO. There are five others that I know of. Paul Nipkow in Germany, John Baird in England, Herbert Ives at the Bell Lab, Ernst Alexanderson at GE and a Russian named Vladimir Zworykin who's working at the Westinghouse Lab in Pittsburgh.

ATKINS. Aren't you afraid they're gonna beat you to it?

PHILO. No sir.

WILKINS. Why not?

SARNOFF. Because they were working on mechanical television, which involved spinning a wheel that had tiny
holes in it. The problem was that to spin it fast enough
to do anything you'd need an engine you could run
at the Formula One Grand Prix of Monaco. Mechanical television wasn't gonna work and Farnsworth knew
that and that's why he was working on electronic television, which Zworykin and the rest of the team told me
was never gonna work but which obviously did. Yeah,
my guys may have called that putt a little early.

ATKINS. You've just named five of the best minds in electricity.

PHILO. Yes sir, I'm surprised they're sticking with it.

SARNOFF. Oh fuck off.

WILKINS. Didn't Zworykin file a patent application for an
electronic system a while back.

SARNOFF. That's right, buddy.

PHILO. Yes sir, four years ago.

SARNOFF. Four years ago.

WILKINS. Why wasn't it granted?

PHILO. It doesn't work.

SARNOFF. It doesn't matter.

WILKINS. Why didn't it work?

PHILO. You've gotta scan the image and break it down into
lines, that's how it's gonna happen. *(pause)* Any more
questions.

ATKINS. Mr. Crocker?

CROCKER. Do you play a musical instrument?

PHILO. I'm sorry?

CROCKER. Do you play a musical instrument of any kind?

PHILO. Yeah, yeah, I play the violin.

CROCKER. No kidding, me too. *(beat)* Not well. My dad
taught me a few songs when I was a kid. Turkey in the
Straw, that sort of thing. You know, I never practiced
much but I liked the lessons. Son, if you go out that
door and make a left, that's my office. Would you wait
there while we talk?

PHILO. Yes sir.

CROCKER. There's a violin back there. Feel free to fiddle around if you get bored.

PHILO. Thank you.

(**PHILO** *exits*)

ATKINS. He's not particularly credentialed in the field.

CROCKER. No one's credentialed in the field.

ATKINS. What he's suggesting defies intuition.

(*Silence. Then...*)

EVERSON. Why did you ask him if he played an instrument?

CROCKER. I'm just struck by the number of times people who are this gifted in math and science also play music. I don't know, they look at a staff, they look at an instrument, it just makes sense to them, they get it.

(*beat*)

All right, here's what I'm gonna do, I'm gonna give him the money. Half. Ten-thousand dollars for the first six months. But he's gotta transmit a picture. If he does, he gets what he needs. If he doesn't, we shake hands and say better luck another day. Leslie, why don't you go get him.

ATKINS. Hang on, Les. Bill, say it does work – and setting aside that at the moment a home television system that may or may not work retails for $10,000 – what do you imagine the practical application being? To say nothing of the marketable one?

CROCKER. The practical and marketable applications of owning the patent on a device that would allow anyone access to all visual information in the world? I'm sure we'll think of something. Les, go get the kid.

(**GORRELL** *starts to head offstage but gets stopped – they all get stopped – by the sound of a Tchaikovsky violin concerto being played offstage.*)

SARNOFF. Yeah, turns out astro-boy was also a concert level violinist.

GORRELL. Mr. Crocker.

CROCKER. Yeah.

GORRELL. Everson and I are in for 3000 dollars.

(LIGHTS CHANGE TO:)

Outside Pem's House

SARNOFF. He tried liquor for the first time when he was in the Navy 'cause he was trying to fit in with guys who couldn't touch his IQ with two hands and a step-ladder so he was happy when Everson and Gorrell produced a celebratory bottle of Bushmills on the train ride home. It was after midnight when the train pulled into Provo, but he got in his car and drove straight to the house of Elma Gardner, who everyone called Pem, and began scouring the ground for a couple of small pebbles.

(**PHILO,** *drunk, is looking around in the dark while muttering to himself –*)

PHILO. Solder and a soldering iron. Filament, filament, filament, filament, some kind of filament wires...

SARNOFF. He'd been in love with Pem for the six months since she scolded him for talking to a group of kids at her church about electro-magnets instead of talking to them about how Jesus had once lived in Utah. When she asked him why he'd changed the topic, he said that he thought there was little evidence to support her theory. She smacked him. And then she kissed him. And I imagine he's been confused ever since.

PHILO. *(to himself)* Varnish, I'm gonna need...coil wires. Copper. These things are gonna heat up, it's gonna matter what kind of varnish.

(He loses his knees for just a second –)

Whoa. All *kinds* a gravity in this area over here.

SARNOFF. She thought he was crazy but she wanted to be with him no matter what absurd future he had in mind for electrons.

PHILO. The most important thing? Your relationship with a glassblower. And how many people can say that?

(He tosses a pebble at a second floor window –)

(quietly:) Pem.

(He tosses another pebble –)

PHILO. Pem.

(The window opens and a tired **MAN** *sticks his head out –)*

MR. GARDNER. Philo?

PHILO. Mr. Gardner.

MR. GARDNER. Watchya doin' out there, son?

PHILO. I'm sorry, sir, I'm turned around, I thought that was Pem's window.

MR. GARDNER. It's pretty late.

*(***MRS. GARDNER** *joins her husband in the window –)*

MRS. GARDNER. Philo?

PHILO. Good evening, Mrs. Gardner, sorry to wake you up.

MRS. GARDNER. Don't be silly, dear. How did it go in San Francisco.

PHILO. It went very well. I just got back and I was hoping to speak to Pem.

(The front door opens and **PEM** *comes out in a bathrobe –)*

PEM. Phil –

PHILO. Pem.

PEM. *Ssh.*

PHILO. Guess what, I parked right on your lawn.

PEM. Phil –

PHILO. Wait, that's not good.

PEM. Are you drunk?

PHILO. Yeah, a little bit. Look –

PEM. *(calling up)* Mom, dad, it's okay, go to bed.

MRS. GARDNER. There's chicken in the ice box.

PHILO. Thank you, ma'am.

PEM. *(scolding)* This is Provo, Utah.

PHILO. How come anytime you're mad at me you tell me where I live?

PEM. Because this is Provo, Utah.

PHILO. I know that, Pem, my mail is delivered here.

PEM. And since you've driven up on my lawn, drunk, at one in the morning and thrown rocks at my parents, is there anything else I do that annoys you?

PHILO. You will leave a cigarette burning in the ashtray without putting it out. So a trail of smoke just kind of curls up to the ceiling for what seems like forever. That doesn't bother you?

PEM. Not as much as you telling me about it.

PHILO. Well, just put that cigarette out with commitment.

PEM. Why are you here right now?

PHILO. I have two reasons and they're both pretty good.

PEM. Phil –

PHILO. The first is that Crocker's gonna finance me.

PEM. *(pause)* What?

PHILO. I'm gonna build it, he's gonna finance me.

PEM. Oh my God.

PHILO. Ten thousand dollars but I have to get a picture in six months or that's it.

PEM. Are you – Oh my God – are you joking? Is this a joke? 'cause your jokes are stupid, Phil.

PHILO. It's real. And my jokes are simply way ahead of their time. Years from now you're going to remember one of my jokes and you're going to laugh, and you're gonna –

PEM. You're going to San Francisco?

PHILO. Yeah. I'm gonna need your brother to come with me and help. And my sister.

PEM. They're gonna be thrilled when they hear the news. They're gonna be – I mean – I can't believe it.

PHILO. Neither can I.

PEM. What was the second one?

PHILO. The second one?

PEM. You said there were two reasons you were here, what was the second one?

PHILO. *(beat)* I don't remember.

PEM. That's because you've been drinking and we're in Provo, Utah, and –

PHILO. I know where we are, can we prioritize?

PEM. Fine.

PHILO. My point is this: I will be working all the time, I mean I have six months to build the image dissector and the receiver so I'll be in the lab the whole time with –

PEM. *(a proud girlfriend)* You're gonna have a lab.

PHILO. And I figure, we'll still be together in San Francisco, I mean we'll be together. We'd have a small apartment and I'll have a small salary, but we could –

PEM. Wait a second.

PHILO. Sure.

PEM. Why will I be in San Francisco?

PHILO. *(pause)* Okay, now I remember what the second one was.

PEM. *(pause)* You're asking me to marry you?

PHILO. Yes, I'm – yes. I'm – yes I am.

PEM. Well...?

PHILO. What?

(*PEM rubs her eyes, bends and over straightens back up in exasperation...*)

PEM. *ASK!*

PHILO. Will you ma –

PEM. Yes.

(*And she throws her arms around him and kisses him...*)

PEM. Wait. When does the six months start?

PHILO. Now. We're gonna leave in the morning. And we're gonna need your mom's chicken.

HARBORD. *(holding up his glass)* To the Patent Pool!

ALL. Here here!

(*LIGHTS CHANGE TO:*)

RCA Party

(Music plays as a cocktail party is underway for radio executives.)

PHILO. A party at the Union Club celebrating the formation of the patent pool – a business arrangement between RCA, AT&T and Westinghouse. Sarnoff hated being in business with AT&T because he hated the company's CFO, Walter Gifford. That's gonna matter later, but for now Sarnoff's consumed with giving people a reason to own a radio.

*(**BETTY**, a pretty woman in her early 20's, comes up to **SARNOFF**.)*

BETTY. Excuse me, Mr. Sarnoff?

SARNOFF. Yeah.

BETTY. I'm Betty Jordan, I'm from the GE secretarial pool and they've assigned me to work with your group.

SARNOFF. Great. Do you know anything about prize fighting?

BETTY. I'm sorry?

SARNOFF. Boxing.

BETTY. No sir.

SARNOFF. Bone up. Four weeks from now we're gonna broadcast a heavyweight title bout from Jersey City between Jack Dempsey and a Frenchman named Georges Carpentier. The signal's gonna travel over 500 miles, that's West Virginia, Ohio, Delaware, we've gotta get some radio sets where the people are. That's what we'll be working on for a while. 7 AM tomorrow?

BETTY. Yes sir.

SARNOFF. Welcome to radio.

*(**JIM HARBORD** calls over –)*

HARBORD. David.

SARNOFF. Yes.

HARBORD. I had lunch with Walter Gifford in the back room at Delmonico's. He tells me you're giving his station manager a hard time over 25 bucks?

SARNOFF. Jim, Walter Gifford runs his radio station like a whore house.

HARBORD. You'd think it'd be more popular then, wouldn't you?

SARNOFF. I wish it were a joke. His guy is on the air telling us it's probably gonna rain on Friday. Then two minutes later he's telling us to remember our umbrellas, and if we don't have one we can pick one up at this place on Queens Boulevard. I do some checking and, yeah, the guy on the air got 25 bucks from the place in Queens to say the name of their store and he did it another two times in the hour.

PARTY GUEST. *(calling over)* Jim!

HARBORD. I'll be right there.

(to SARNOFF)

What's the problem?

SARNOFF. Well first of all, now I don't know if it's really gonna rain on Friday or not.

HARBORD. A hundred people were listening.

SARNOFF. Gimme three years, it'll be a hundred million, and then –

HARBORD. Enjoy the party, David, it's a party.

SARNOFF. Credibility can't be regained. You lose it and you're in the circus.

(HARBORD walks away into the party.)

HARBORD. I like the circus.

SARNOFF. *(calling after)* Everybody likes the circus, that's not the – ah fuck it.

LIZETTE. Watch your language, Mr. Sarnoff.

(LIZETTE, who speaks with a light French accent, has come up behind SARNOFF with two drinks.)

SARNOFF. I'm sorry, honey, I didn't see you there. I was talking to Jim.

LIZETTE. You were angry.

SARNOFF. Walter Gifford is allowing people to pay money to advertise during informational programming.

LIZETTE. How long is this feud going to go on?

SARNOFF. 17 years.

LIZETTE. Why?

SARNOFF. *(to the audience)* U.S. patents last 17 years.

LIZETTE. My darling, advertising during informational programming is not the reason you don't like Walter Gifford.

SARNOFF. I promise you Liz, it's business and nothing else.

LIZETTE. I've been talking to Tatiana Zworykin. Her husband is working on a kinescope.

SARNOFF. That's right.

LIZETTE. What's a kinescope?

SARNOFF. It's…well I guess you'd have to call it – what – a television receiver. It's like a radio receiver but instead of receiving a sound wave, it receives a light image. Also it doesn't work.

LIZETTE. What do you mean it receives a light image?

SARNOFF. Just what it sounds like.

LIZETTE. You're trying to transmit a picture?

SARNOFF. Well I'm not, Zworykin is, and some guys in Europe, but it doesn't work.

LIZETTE. You mean *project* an image.

SARNOFF. No I mean transmit an image. You'd be standing in another room and you could watch a kinescope and see this party.

LIZETTE. That's incredible.

SARNOFF. Except for one thing?

LIZETTE. What?

SARNOFF. It doesn't work.

LIZETTE. Will it?

SARNOFF. What.

LIZETTE. Work.

SARNOFF. Television?

LIZETTE. Yes.

SARNOFF. I don't see how, but if television gets invented it's not gonna get invented by a guy at Westinghouse, it's gonna get invented by RCA.

PHILO. *(calling)* Cliffy!

(LIGHTS CHANGE TO GREEN STREET LAB)

(Where **PHILO, PEM** *and* **AGNES** *are greeting* **CLIFF,** *with* **STAN** *waiting to be introduced.)*

CLIFF. Phil. Hey, Pem. Hey, Agnes. We've been sweeping up the place. Welcome to your lab.

STAN. Mr. Farnsworth, I'm Stan Willis.

PHILO. From Cal Tech.

STAN. Mr. Crocker's office hired me to help you.

PHILO. Well, I'll take all you can spare. When did you graduate?

STAN. I haven't, I'm a junior, they're giving me class credit.

PHILO. Okay. Well that's my wife, Pem.

PEM. Nice to meet you.

STAN. Ma'am.

PHILO. And her brother, Cliff Gardner and that's my sister Agnes.

STAN. How do you do.

AGNES. Nice to meet you.

CLIFF. How did I beat you here?

PHILO. We had car trouble.

CLIFF. What happened?

PHILO. Agnes drove into a salt flat.

AGNES. You were yammering about birdseed.

PHILO. I was yammering about Birdseye. Clarence Birdseye. Stan, did you see in the paper today?

STAN. Yeah.

PHILO. *(to* **CLIFF***)* This guy's gonna flash freeze vegetables. Freeze them in an instant so they retain their cellular structure.

AGNES. Who cares?

PHILO. Anyone who eats food.

CLIFF. You know, Phil –

(to **PEM**)

Should I ask him now?

PEM. Go ahead.

PHILO. What?

CLIFF. Pem said you were gonna need glass tubes and since money's tight I thought I could teach myself how to make them and maybe cut out the expense of a glass-blower. *(beat)* I want to be a part of this, Phil. I'm not smart enough to, you know, I'm not like you –

PHILO. You're plenty smart.

CLIFF. I can learn how to make glass tubes.

PHILO. Glassblowing's hard and it's dangerous. These guys apprentice for a long time and I'm looking for them to make me one that's gonna be hard to make.

(**HARLAN HONN** *enters*)

HARLAN. Mr. Farnsworth?

PHILO. *(to **CLIFF**)* You are gonna be a part of it.

(to **HARLAN**)

Yes.

HARLAN. I'm Harlan Honn, I'm in the lab next door.

PHILO. Nice to meet you.

HARLAN. I'm working on new methods of refrigeration.

PHILO. What's wrong with the old methods?

HARLAN. If it leaks, there's a risk to consumers that they might die from the poisonous gas that's emitted.

PHILO. Well you better get on that then. Hey, Stan, do you have a place to live?

STAN. I was just gonna get a room down at the Y.

PHILO. We're gonna rent an apartment across the Bay, why don't you stay with us and save a couple of bucks.

STAN. Gee, thanks.

PHILO. *(to* **PEM** *)* Is that okay?

PEM. You betchya, Phil. Just me, you, my brother, your sister and a junior from Cal Tech. Aggie, let's go find a four bedroom apartment for 30 dollars a month.

PHILO. Hey see if you can find one that has a nice view of the –

PEM. Shut up.

PHILO. You bet.

> *(*PEM *and* AGNES *exit.)*

HARLAN. Well if you need anything I'm in the lab next door. If you need any equipment or another pair of hands.

PHILO. I wouldn't want to distract you from what you're doing.

HARLAN. Refrigeration? Please distract me.

> *(*HARLAN *exits.)*

PHILO. Okay. Stan, what do you know about moving pictures.

STAN. I know a film projector has to move a series of photographs past the human eye at a speed of 16 frames per second to fool the brain into thinking it's watching fluid movement.

PHILO. Yeah we're gonna try something a little different. You go get us a generator, Cliff and I are gonna start building a lab.

SARNOFF. So now he's got his team. His brother-in-law, a 19-year-old kid and a refrigerator repairman. I mention this because 50 PhD's at Bell, AT&T and Westinghouse told me that what was about to happen was impossible.

ACTOR #1. United States Patent Application 1-773-980, made by Philo T. Farnsworth of Berkley, California.

> *(And now, while we watch* **PHILO, CLIFF, STAN, HARLAN, PEM** *and* **AGNES** *come on and off, assembling various parts of the lab which is getting more and crowded, lights come up on a* **CHORUS** *of cast members reciting sections of Philo's patent application. They should speak over one another, sometimes three, four or five voices at once.)*

ACTOR #2. This apparatus relates to the apparatus and process for the transmission of a moving image to a distance.

ACTOR #3. The transmission is by electricity –

ACTOR #2. Heretofore attempts have been made to transmit an image. These prior attempts have generally embodied a method or apparatus –

ACTOR #4. – in which each particular elemental area –

ACTOR #1. – that the human eye will retain a picture is of such short duration that the conversion of the light shades of the original image of the object to electricity and reconversion of electricity to light –

ACTOR #5. – cross section of such electronic discharge from the place, in which each portion of the cross section will correspond in electrical intensity with intensity of light imposed on –

ACTOR #3. – developed, fluctuating in intensity to the variations of the light current transmitted without the necessity –

ACTOR #2. Figure 2 is a diagrammatic view of the television receiver. Figure 3 is –

ACTOR #4. Figure 16 is a perspective view of a biaxial crystal showing the refraction of –

ACTOR #1. Figure 22 –

ACTOR #3. Figure 31 –

ACTOR #5. Figure 45 –

SARNOFF. In testimony whereof, I have heretofore set my hand. Philo T. Farnsworth.

PHILO. All right, let's try it.

> (**STAN** *flips a toggle and BOOMPH!, the whole thing blows up in an electrical surge.* **CLIFF, STAN, HARLAN** *and* **EVERSON** *and* **GORRELL,** *who came to watch the equipment test, jump back immediately.* **PHILO** *doesn't move, he just stands expressionless.* **HARLAN** *and* **CLIFF** *grab buckets of sand and throw it on the small fire that's started while* **STAN** *goes to the generator.)*

STAN. It was a power surge, Phil.

HARLAN. It was the generator?

SARNOFF. The one thing in the room they hadn't built from scratch.

PHILO. It was the *generator*?!

STAN. I'm sorry, sir, that was me.

PHILO. Don't worry about it.

GORRELL. Don't worry about it? *(beat)* Do you have anything to show for our money?

PHILO. *(pause)* The table works.

GORRELL. You have five weeks left.

> (**EVERSON** *and* **GORRELL** *exit*)

PHILO. All right, well…we'll fix the generator, but once we do, is there a photoelectric material that's a better conductor than potassium?

HARLAN. Sodium.

STAN. We tried sodium.

HARLAN. Topaz?

PHILO. No.

HARLAN. No, could use willemite?

PHILO. I was thinking of cesium.

HARLAN. Yeah, but where are we gonna get it?

PHILO. Don't they use cesium pellets in the tubes that they put in radio kits? That you see in the Sears Roebuck catalogue? Little cesium pellets?

STAN. They do, I had one, but they're tiny.

PHILO. Yeah, we're gonna have to go to every hobby store in the city and buy every radio kit they've got.

SARNOFF. They spent all day buying radio kits, then all night smashing the tubes open with a hammer, emptying the pellets out and grinding them into a paste. The change to cesium was gonna help but the selenium hadn't been his problem and he knew that. His problem was that no one had been able to build him the glass tube he wanted. He'd be through five different glassblowers. Two of them produced tube after tube that broke apart the moment they cooled, two others turned down the job outright and the fifth was doing the best he could. It was after midnight and Crocker was coming to the lab the next morning. His six months were up. He sat on the roof with a glass and a bottle of Bushmills.

(LIGHTS UP ON ROOF)

(where **PHILO***'s standing)*

PHILO. *(to himself)* Cesium'll send a spray…maybe manipulated through…rubidium…

PEM. *(offstage)* Phil, you out there?

PHILO. Yeah.

*(***PEM*** comes out on the roof.)*

PEM. You want anything?

PHILO. No thanks.

PEM. You want your violin?

PHILO. No, I'm fine.

PEM. *(pause)* You wanna hear something funny? Bill Crocker says there's a correlation between music and science.

PHILO. Music is what mathematics does on a Saturday night.

PEM. Stan and Harlan are in there trying to rebuild it again.

PHILO. We don't have it.

PEM. We will.

PHILO. Not by tomorrow morning.

PEM. Then you'll get more money from someone else. This isn't the end.

PHILO. I'm sure you're right.

PEM. But if it doesn't work I'm not gonna make love to you until it does.

*(***PHILO*** smiles.)*

PEM. No, I'm serious.

HARLAN. *(from inside)* Phil!

PHILO. Then I'm screwed.

PEM. Not until you get a picture you're not so let's go.

(LIGHTS UP ON LAB)

HARLAN. *(calling)* Phil!

(STAN and HARLAN are looking at something with great interest as CLIFF stands nearby and PHILO and PEM come in from the roof.)

PHILO. What are you guys doing?

HARLAN. I think you better look at this.

PHILO. What is it?

STAN. Cliff made it.

(STAN holds out a glass tube...PHILO looks at it...)

PHILO. *(to CLIFF)* You made this?

CLIFF. He let me watch for a few weeks, and then he showed me some things...and you've talked about what it needed and what it was –

PHILO. When did you do this?

CLIFF. The first two were no good but I did this one yesterday. And then I let it cool. I did it during lunches and at –

PEM. *(is this for real?)* Phil?

PHILO. Cliff made a cathode tube. *(beat)* This is the one we're using, we gotta tear this thing apart and rebuild it again.

STAN. You know there won't be time to test it before they get here in the morning.

PHILO. Have any of the tests worked?

STAN. No.

PHILO. Then what does it matter. Let's go.

(A SOUND CUE. A low, pulsing, tension-building beat begins underneath)

SARNOFF. Harlan bumped into the camera, right?

PHILO. Yeah.

SARNOFF. It ended up aimed at the drafting table?

PHILO. Yeah.

SARNOFF. And Pem had been making notes in the lab notebooks so the desk lamp was on.

PHILO. Yeah.

SARNOFF. That's pretty good luck.

PHILO. You think I got lucky?

SARNOFF. *(beat)* No.

PHILO. I didn't think so.

GORRELL. Are we ready?

PHILO. In a second.

SARNOFF. The room was divided in half by a black curtain. On one side was the camera aimed at a triangle on a rod which would swing back and forth like a pendulum to demonstrate motion. On the other side of the curtain was a receiver.

(The triangle and the camera are offstage. **CROCKER** *and his lieutenants,* **ATKINS** *and* **WILKINS,** *as well as* **EVERSON** *and* **GORRELL, HARLAN, CLIFF** *and* **STAN** *are beginning to gather near the television set. A* **PHOTOGRAPHER** *joins the group. The pulsing sound continues to build.)*

AGNES. *(to* **PHILO***)* Good luck.

*(***PEM** *comes over and joins her husband.)*

PEM. The triangle's moving.

*(***HARLAN** *comes in.)*

PHILO. *(to* **HARLAN***)* The triangle's moving?

HARLAN. Yeah, but listen –

PHILO. *(to the group)* All right, gentlemen, the triangle I showed you before is moving now, you can go to the other side of the curtain if you want and take a look.

(to **HARLAN***)*

Yeah.

HARLAN. *(quietly)* Listen.

PHILO. What?

GORRELL. What?

HARLAN. Nothing.

SARNOFF. Harlan had bumped into the image dissector while he was back there setting the triangle. He tried to check for damage but there wasn't time, that's what he was trying to tell him.

PHILO. Stan?

SARNOFF. He started the current.

PHILO. It's gonna warm up a second.

(The pulsing continues to build.)

SARNOFF. And the viewing screen filled with electronic fog.

(HARLAN and STAN look at each other and drop their heads in disappointment.)

SARNOFF. Nothing. Nothing but the electronic fog and a cloudy, wavy line running up the middle.

(After a moment…)

ATKINS. Damn.

CROCKER. It was a good effort, son. You've got nothing to be ashamed of.

EVERSON. He's right, Phil, you gave it a good shot.

SARNOFF. He wasn't hearing them, though. He was just staring at the electronic fog with the cloudy, wavy line running up the middle.

HARLAN. Phil.

PHILO. Hang on.

(PHILO's moving closer the screen. He sees something.)

HARLAN. I bumped the camera before.

PHILO. Hang on.

HARLAN. When I was back there setting the triangle. I turned and my back hit the –

PHILO. Hang on.

HARLAN. I'm sure I hit the image dissector, something coulda come loose. If everybody can stay for a little while, we can –

PHILO. *(caught in the emotion and calling out much louder then he needs to)* Pem!

PEM. He's right, if he knocked something loose –

PHILO. Did you leave a cigarette burning in the ashtray on the drafting table?

PEM. *(beat)* What?

PHILO. Did you leave a cigarette burning in the ashtray?!

PEM. Well what does it matter if I –

(**PHILO** *runs offstage to see then runs right back on*)

PHILO. You didn't break it Harlan, you moved it.

(pointing to the TV)

That's the smoke.

("What?" "What?" "Huh?" "The wavy line?," "What's he – ")

PHILO. That's the smoke.

CROCKER. Hang on.

(**CROCKER** *goes offstage, comes back and looks at the screen.)*

CROCKER. *(beat – to everyone)* It is.

HARLAN. Oh my God.

ATKINS. I'll be goddamned.

WILKINS. Shit.

EVERSON. It is, that's the cigarette – Leslie, look at this, that's the cigarette smoke.

GORRELL. Oh my God.

PHILO. *(shouting)* Cliff! We got a picture!

(And now the place has erupted into whoops and hollers and applause. People are going offstage and coming back to check the monitor, clapping each other on the back –)

CLIFF. We got a picture.

PEM. *PHILLL!*

(*She hugs him and kisses him.*)

PHILO. Showing off for women is a powerful incentive.

STAN. There it is!

CLIFF. Look at that.

STAN. That's a goddam television picture!

PHOTOGRAPHER. Mr. Farnsworth?

PHILO. Yeah.

PHOTOGRAPHER. Face front please for the *San Francisco Chronicle.*

(*Boomph! He flashes a picture and the stage goes black except for a pinspot on* **PHILO.**)

(*We hear a* **RADIO VOICE.**)

RADIO VOICE. Razor Blade Michigan Pattern Ax: One-dollar, eighty-five cents.

PHILO. (*to the audience*) The Jack Dempsey/Georges Carpentier title bout was billed as a battle between good and evil with Carpentier being good and Dempsey being evil. I can't remember why.

RADIO VOICE. Fulton Razor Blade Double Bit Michigan Pattern Ax: two-dollars, forty cents.

PHILO. It didn't matter – Dempsey would win in a late round knockout – what mattered was that this was the first sporting event ever broadcast and radio was about to get launched like a Hercules rocket, which you'd think would make Sarnoff happy since he was the mastermind behind every square inch of it.

RADIO VOICE. Fulton Hunter's Hatchet: ninety-five cents.

(*LIGHTS CHANGE TO RCA CONFERENCE ROOM*)

(**SARNOFF,** *along with* **WACHTEL, SIMMS** *and a few other* **EXECUTIVES,** *are listening to a radio commercial.*)

PHILO. He's not happy, though, 'cause right now he's listening to Walter Gifford's radio which at the moment is broadcasting –

(**PHILO** *points –*)

RADIO VOICE. Handy Hand Saws, 24 inches: Two-dollars, thirty-five cents. Universal Fuse Plugs, made to fit *all* universal hollow ware: One-dollar, ten-cents. All this at Robinson's Family Hardware, located at 77th Street and Broadway, open six days from 9 AM to 6 PM. Fulton Perforated Lance Tooth Saw –

SARNOFF. How long does this go on?

WACHTEL. Ten minutes.

RADIO VOICE. Lufkin Flat-End Three Quarter-Inch and Half-Inch –

WACHTEL. He's selling ten-minute blocks of time for 50 dollars.

SARNOFF. I asked him not to do that.

SIMMS. You asked him not to have his people take money under the table.

SARNOFF. Did he think that meant I wanted him to take it over the table?

WACHTEL. Well it's his station, David, he can –

SARNOFF. Hang on.

RADIO VOICE. Reversible type handle ratchet wrench: Seventy-five cents.

SARNOFF. You know if you listen carefully, you can hear the sound of people throwing their radio sets out the window, buying a phonograph and shooting me in the fucking head.

RADIO VOICE. General Purpose Wheelbarrow –

SARNOFF. You can't do this, fellas, it's not what it's for.

PHILO. Damn. If only there was a powerful person in broadcasting with the courage of his convictions who could do something about this.

SARNOFF. *(to PHILO)* Well I assume that was meant for me there, Billy-Bob, so I'll just say that I've spent more time and effort than anyone ever trying to make television and radio informative, entertaining and sophisticated.

PHILO. Job well done.

SARNOFF. The picture you got was of no practical value, you needed too much light.

PHILO. Yeah, the first time Orville and Wilbur flew Kitty Hawk it went about 17 feet but I think we're pretty happy it did.

SARNOFF. There was no way it was gonna get approved by the Commerce Department for commercial use in the state it was –

PHILO. Zworykin didn't have a picture at all.

SARNOFF. He solved your light problem. He solved your light problem and he'd filed a patent four years earlier –

(to the EXECUTIVES)

– and can somebody tell me what the fuck you've got in a hardware store you need ten minutes to sell me?! Is there clairvoyance in this store?!

RADIO VOICE. All this at Robinson's Family Hardware Store, located at 77th and Broad –

(HARBORD enters.)

HARBORD. Good morning.

ALL. Good morning.

HARBORD. Tex Rickert's promoting the fight as good versus evil.

SIMMS. And which one's which?

HARBORD. Jack Dempsey's evil. Wife beater, draft dodger –

PHILO. That's why. That's why, I couldn't remember why.

WACHTEL. Plus he's got that face.

SIMMS. And Carpentier's our hero?

HARBORD. French fighter pilot, he speaks French.

SARNOFF. He *is* French.

HARBORD. The French fighter pilot versus the Manhattan Mauler.

SARNOFF. Manassa, he's the Manassa Mauler. Manassa, Colorado. Jim, we've got a problem.

HARBORD. Hang on. Is the signal gonna travel 500 miles, is this confirmed?

WACHTEL. A 50,000 watt transmitter that was going by train to the Navy Department in DC was diverted to a Lackawanna Railroad shed a tenth of a mile from the arena.

HARBORD. Who got that done?

ALL. *(who else)* Sarnoff.

SARNOFF. Jim –

WACHTEL. J.P.'s daughter, Anne Morgan, she was recruited to set up charity events all up and down the coast.

SIMMS. They write a check to a good cause, they come to a house and have champagne and oysters and listen to the fight on the radio.

WACHTEL. All in, we're expecting 200,000 people to be listening.

HARBORD. This broadcast is gonna make us bigger than Westinghouse, David, what do you have to say for yourself?

SARNOFF. I just listened to ten minutes of information about a hardware store on WEAF.

HARBORD. That's small potatoes.

SARNOFF. No, no, it's a very big potato.

HARBORD. It's Gifford's station, leave him alone.

SARNOFF. It's our equipment, which no one will buy if the airwaves are filled with the price of a three-quarter inch drill bit. We're gonna be responsible for entertaining and informing a nation and we don't have an engineer in Schenectady or an executive in New York who knows anything about that.

SIMMS. David –

SARNOFF. We need to create a new company, Jim, a subdivision. The American Radio Group or the The Public Radio Network – something – and bring in people who are experts at reporting information and events, experts in education, culture, public affairs and leaders in forming...

SIMMS. What?

SARNOFF. *(beat) Taste!*

WACHTEL. Who gets the final call on what public taste should be, to say nothing of education and information?

SARNOFF. We do this thing right and it's us.

HARBORD. Let's get through the Manassa Mauler and then we can talk about being tastemakers. Thank you. David, would you stay a moment?

SARNOFF. Yes sir.

(As the room begins clearing, SARNOFF scribbles something on his legal pad and slides it down the table.)

SARNOFF. *(continued)* Jerry, do me a favor, just for the hell of it, ask legal to run a clearance on this trademark and see if anyone's using it.

JERRY. Sure.

PHILO. He'd scribbled some names on the pad – "American Radio Group," "American Radio Network," "Public Radio Corporation" – but he'd crossed those out. On the bottom of the page he'd circled his winner. The National Broadcasting Company.

(The room is empty now except for SARNOFF and HARBORD.)

HARBORD. All right, what's your beef with Walter Gifford other than the obvious.

SARNOFF. It's got nothing to do with that, it's business.

HARBORD. Good.

SARNOFF. But AT&T's gotta get out of radio.

HARBORD. Gifford's not gonna take a back seat to RCA.

SARNOFF. I don't want them to take a back seat, I want 'em out of the car.

HARBORD. David –

SARNOFF. Let me buy the audion tube.

HARBORD. It's gonna cost too much money.

SARNOFF. It's gonna make more. It's gonna replace the crystal and it's what's gonna make music sound good. We'll control it, we have to control the patents and we shouldn't be paying royalties, we should be collecting them. The next time you talk to Gifford, and I think it should be soon, you gotta make it clear –

HARBORD. I won't be talking to Gifford.

SARNOFF. Why not?

HARBORD. All the rumors you've heard are true. They've been talking to me for a few weeks and they made it official last night.

SARNOFF. You're gonna go work for Herbert Hoover?

(HARBORD nods "yeah.")

SARNOFF. Congratulations, Jim. You're gonna want to try not to screw that up.

HARBORD. Yeah.

SARNOFF. Who's taking your place? Ted? You should think about Charles.

HARBORD. It's you. You're being named at a press conference on Monday.

(SARNOFF is frozen…)

SARNOFF. *(pause)* What?

HARBORD. You're gonna want to try not to screw that up.

(HARBORD exits, passing LIZETTE on her way into the conference room.)

HARBORD. 'Afternoon, Lizette.

LIZETTE. Good afternoon, Mr. Harbord. *(beat)* David?

SARNOFF. Liz.

LIZETTE. Are we still having lunch?

SARNOFF. Hm?

LIZETTE. David, is everything all right?

SARNOFF. Yeah. I'm the president of RCA.

PHILO. It was a significant accomplishment. After three weeks in his new job, it was time to take a meeting.

SARNOFF. *(calling)* Betty?

BETTY. *(entering)* Yes sir.

SARNOFF. I'd like you to set up lunch with Walter Gifford.

BETTY. Yes sir, at his earliest convenience?

SARNOFF. No, I don't care if it's convenient.

(LIGHTS CHANGE TO RESTAURANT)

(A power lunch spot filled with Manhattan's top executives)

MAITRE D'. Good afternoon, Mr. Sarnoff.

SARNOFF. Good afternoon, Tony.

MAITRE D'. Mr. Gifford's already here.

SARNOFF. Thank you.

MAITRE D'. Dry martini.

SARNOFF. Thanks very much.

(*SARNOFF goes to* **GIFFORD** *'s table and sits.*)

GIFFORD. David.

SARNOFF. Walter.

GIFFORD. I was gonna give you another two minutes and then order lunch.

SARNOFF. I apologize.

GIFFORD. If you're gonna be a captain of industry you're gonna have to learn that captains of industry don't like to wait for their fucking wives much less the guy who's been president of RCA for three weeks.

SARNOFF. I was tuned to your radio station last night.

GIFFORD. I'm glad to hear it.

SARNOFF. There was a man named H.M. Blackwell and he was identified as a representative of the Queensboro Corporation.

GIFFORD. I gotta tell you, David, ordinarily I'm not someone who gets summoned to lunch meetings.

SARNOFF. This guy, Blackwell, he chatted about the carefree life in the suburbs, free from the hustle of the city.

GIFFORD. Yeah.

SARNOFF. And ended by urging us to – "hurry to the apartment house near the green fields for the community life and friendly atmosphere that Nathaniel Hawthorne advocated."

GIFFORD. What can I do for you?

SARNOFF. You know the name of the apartment house near the green fields?

GIFFORD. David –

SARNOFF. Hawthorne Estates, an apartment complex owned by – ?

GIFFORD. Oh stop your –

SARNOFF. The Queensboro Corporation.

GIFFORD. It wasn't a direct pitch.

SARNOFF. We'll set aside he was blowing Nathaniel Hawthorne all to hell, you don't think people know when they're being sold an apartment in Jackson Heights? You've got a 13-year-old girl from Wilkes-Barre singing Jerome Kern –

GIFFORD. I like Jerome Kern.

SARNOFF. So do I and I think other people will too if his songs are sung by singers.

GIFFORD. What the hell is this lunch about?

SARNOFF. It's a courtesy.

GIFFORD. You're being courteous right now.

SARNOFF. Yes.

GIFFORD. How?

SARNOFF. By telling you in person that your company isn't in the radio business anymore.

GIFFORD. How are you gonna swing that?

SARNOFF. I already did. Your boss is getting 10% of RCA preferred stock.

GIFFORD. What's RCA getting?

SARNOFF. The audion tube.

GIFFORD. *(pause)* You *bought* the audion tube?

SARNOFF. Yes.

GIFFORD. You gave away 10% of your company for the audion tube?

SARNOFF. I'll tell you, it would've been a steal at twice the price.

GIFFORD. And what are you saying, you're saying – you're saying you're not gonna license it out, that's what you're saying now?

SARNOFF. Of course we're gonna license it out.

GIFFORD. Good.

SARNOFF. Just not to you.

GIFFORD. I'll take this to an arbitrator.

SARNOFF. I know you will.

GIFFORD. You're a cocksucker.

SARNOFF. I've been told that before.

GIFFORD. You think if radio's bad once in a while that people won't start listening, that's your nightmare?

SARNOFF. I don't know which is my nightmare. That radio's bad and people don't start listening or that radio's bad and they do. Either way, I'll take my chances with the arbitrator.

GIFFORD. Alright, David?

SARNOFF. Yes.

GIFFORD. David.

SARNOFF. Yes sir.

GIFFORD. I don't like the publicity, David, is there any way to avoid that?

SARNOFF. Sure.

GIFFORD. I'm serious.

SARNOFF. Me too. We can fix it up right now and everybody's happy and I license you the audion tube and you keep your stations. We can do it right now, it's simple.

GIFFORD. How?

SARNOFF. Give me the name of one Jew who works at AT&T.

(**GIFFORD** *stares at him...*)

SARNOFF. *(beat)* One Jew. Anywhere. Doesn't have to be an executive. Bookkeeping, the switchboard –

GIFFORD. *(getting up)* This lunch is over.

(**GIFFORD** *exits. The* **WAITER** *comes over and sets* **SAR- NOFF**'s *martini down.*)

SARNOFF. Thank you. You can take Mr. Gifford's drink, he won't be back.

WAITER. Yes sir. Will you be staying?

SARNOFF. Yeah, I'm not going anywhere.

PHILO. In fact he was just gettin' warmed up. He bought the audion tube, he bought the Frequency Modulation band from the great Edwin Armstrong and he launched the NBC Radio Network. He dictated memo after memo and gave speech after speech discussing the civic responsibilities of the custodians of mass communication.

(LIGHTS UP ON SARNOFF'S OFFICE)

(where he's dictating to **BETTY***)*

SARNOFF. When you can transmit the human voice into the home, when you can make the home attuned to what is going on in the rest of the world, you've tapped a new source of influence and the possibility that we can raise ourselves up culturally, spiritually, intellectually and economically. It is my regrettable obligation to tell you that RCA does not own the airwaves.

(We hear an appreciative laugh and applause as the–)

(LIGHTS CHANGE TO PODIUM)

(Where **SARNOFF** *is delivering a speech)*

SARNOFF. We don't own the airwaves anymore than we own the air and it's only a matter of time before somebody taps Congress on the shoulder and reminds them of that, and friends, that's going to be bad for business. Radio stations should be run like public libraries.

PHILO. And anyone who knew anything was buying RCA stock.

ACTOR #1. RCA's up a point and a half.

ACTOR #2. RCA stock sets new record!

ACTOR #3. 64 and three-eights.

ACTOR #4. It's at 71 and 3/8ths.

ACTOR #5. General Motors puts radios in cars!

ACTOR #6. I sold it at 77.

ACTOR #7. It's up to 85.

ACTOR #1. 91.

ACTOR #8. 93.

ACTOR #6. 97 dollars a share.

ACTOR #4. Up two points.

ACTOR #7. Up three and a half.

ACTOR #3. One hundred and twenty-nine dollars.

PHILO. If you'd invested $10,000 in RCA the day before the Dempsey fight, three years later you'd be a millionaire. When his bosses at GE showed him the plans for new office space in the Art Deco building being constructed at 30 Rockefeller Center, Sarnoff took a red pen and circled a wing of offices on a particular floor that would be used for his team. *(beat)* He called it Radio City.

WACHTEL. We would acquire all the assets of Victor Talking Machines –

(LIGHTS CHANGE TO CONFERENCE ROOM)

(A meeting is underway.)

WACHTEL. – including your manufacturing plant in Camden which we would annex to our own. And, uh…well it should go without saying that we're also acquiring… uh…

SARNOFF. *(pause)* The dog.

WACHTEL. The dog.

SARNOFF. What's his name?

WACHTEL. Nipper.

SARNOFF. People have confidence in the dog.

PHILO. Once a week, a junior executive named Ridley would run to a newsstand on Lexington Avenue that sold out of town newspapers. On this day he drops a quarter in a dish and picks up *The Chicago Daily News, The Washington Evening Star, The Philadelphia Ledger…* and a week and a half old copy of *The San Francisco Chronicle.*

(LIGHTS CHANGE TO SARNOFF'S OFFICE)

(RIDLEY enters with a newspaper.)

RIDLEY. Betty –

BETTY. You're out of breath.

RIDLEY. I ran here.

BETTY. What's the matter?

RIDLEY. I need to see him.

BETTY. He's just getting out of a meeting with the guys from Victor, what in the world has happened?

RIDLEY. A guy in San Francisco –

(SARNOFF enters.)

SARNOFF. Betty.

RIDLEY. David, the newspaper –

SARNOFF. It's done, we've got a phonograph company.

RIDLEY. There's an item on the front page of *The San Francisco Chronicle.*

SARNOFF. No listen to this. The symbol's going to be a dog who thinks he hears his master's voice coming from a gramophone.

RIDLEY. A guy named Philo Farnsworth –

SARNOFF. Calm down.

RIDLEY. A guy named Philo Farnsworth –

SARNOFF. What's the name?

RIDLEY. Philo.

SARNOFF. Spell it.

RIDLEY. P-H-I-L-O. He's been working on television.

SARNOFF. Who isn't?

RIDLEY. No, he's been working on electronic television.

SARNOFF. Well lemme know when he gets a picture 'cause Zworykin says it can't be done and he's been trying most of his life. Why's *The San Francisco Chronicle* interested in this guy?

RIDLEY. He got a picture.

(And now we start to hear the same low, slow-building pulsing sound that was under the scene where Philo got the first picture...)

SARNOFF. *(pause)* What are you talking about?

(**RIDLEY** *hands him the paper.* **SARNOFF** *reads…the pulsing continues.*)

SARNOFF. Betty, get the department heads here. Engineering, commercial, legal. Get the patent cops.

BETTY. Yes sir, when?

SARNOFF. Now, Betty. The goddam paper's a week old.

(LIGHTS CHANGE TO CONFERENCE ROOM)

(Where the department heads are entering.)

JAMES. Well the way I read it, Farnsbrook's asking for proprietary status on three separate patents.

SARNOFF. Farnsworth. Philo Farnsworth.

JAMES. The first is for something called an electric oscillator system. The second is for what he's calling an image dissector and the third is for the television receiving system.

LENNOX. You're worrying about nothing, David.

SOLOMON. *(reading)* "In my laboratory at the present time I have a system in operation which requires a wave band of only six kilocycles to carry the images from the transmitter to the receiver," Mr. Farnsworth continued.

LENNOX. Much ado about nothing.

SOLOMON. *(reading)* "It is perfectly possible to reduce this wave band to five kilocycles so it can be sent out by regular broadcasting stations. I expect the receiving device will be able to be sold at retail for under $300."

SARNOFF. How is it possible, I mean how is it *fucking possible* that RCA is finding out about this from the *The San Francisco Chronicle*?

LENNOX. David –

SARNOFF. How long before the Commerce Department approves it for commercial use?

LENNOX. This is what I'm trying to tell you. It's a very weak picture he got and to get a stronger one he'd need lights too hot to –

SARNOFF. But that's just engineering, right?

LENNOX. Maybe.

SARNOFF. He could have a practical picture in a year?

LENNOX. He's got very serious light problems to solve.

SARNOFF. And I'm asking isn't that just engineering and how long will it take to –

SIMMS. An under-funded, under-staffed, ill-educated Mormon in a one-room lab?

SARNOFF. He got this far somehow, he didn't build the thing out of bibles and moonshine. Howard, is there any part of a television operating system he's not going to own the exclusive rights to?

HOWARD. He made the console out of pine.

SARNOFF. So you're saying he's not going to own the patent on wood.

WACHTEL. Why don't we just make him an offer on it.

SARNOFF. We can't.

WACHTEL. Why not?

SARNOFF. We can't.

WACHTEL. David –

SARNOFF/PHILO. *(at the same time)* If we make him an offer it means he invented television!

WACHTEL. Offer him a hundred-thousand, offer it to him in stock, he'll take it.

SARNOFF. He might, but if he doesn't that's the ball game. And a year from now, when he solves whatever problem he's having with light and the thing gets approved for sale, he's gonna own General Electric and anything else he wants to buy. *(beat)* We can't buy his system 'cause that'd mean he invented it and he didn't, we did, it's just that ours doesn't work yet. Howard, if Zworykin can get a good picture before Farnsworth, if he can get it first, can he revisit his 1923 patent application and seek priority of invention?

HOWARD. Yes.

SARNOFF. What's our budget for television research?

SIMMS. $50,000.

SARNOFF. Give Zworykin two hundred thousand and double his staff. Call our people at Corning and tell 'em he gets all the glass he needs.

WACHTEL. David, can I say something please, before we start doing things that might make us look foolish in the eyes of, at the very least, our shareholders? It's a gadget, it's a parlor trick for a couple of rich people. It's something you show at the World's Fair.

SARNOFF. You're wrong.

WACHTEL. The thing's a monstrosity, David. It's huge and unsightly. Think of a person's home, where the hell are they gonna put it?

SARNOFF. Where they used to put their radio. *(beat)* All right, that's all.

(Everyone exits. BETTY enters)

BETTY. *(beat)* Can I get you anything?

SARNOFF. When it rains it pours, Betty.

BETTY. I'm sorry?

SARNOFF. Gifford's gonna sue us in Federal Court. I have a hunch the Court's gonna end up calling our patent pool by a different name.

BETTY. What are they gonna call it?

SARNOFF. An illegal monopoly. And a report from the Treasury Department says that as of today, more people have invested in radio than own radios.

BETTY. What does that mean?

SARNOFF. It means our stock might be over-valued and headed for what's called an adjustment. A little like the adjustment the French gave to Louis the 16th. *(beat)* I'm sorry, you came in here and you asked me something.

BETTY. Just if I could get you anything.

SARNOFF. No, thank you. You can go home.

BETTY. *(beat)* You know, for what it's worth, my father used to say, when a string of things went bad, he used to say well at least you know nothing's gonna happen next.

(BETTY exits. SARNOFF's now standing alone in the same pool of light that he was at the beginning of the play)

SARNOFF. *(to the audience)* And I remember thinking that was funny. 'cause my father used to say something always happens next.

(CURTAIN.)

End of Act One

ACT TWO

(Light comes up on **PHILO** *as the scrim rises.)*

PHILO. This is a true story. Early on the morning of October 29th, 1929, a huge flock of blackbirds and starlings, in the middle of their migratory route south, landed in front of City Hall Plaza in New York. They actually stopped traffic on Fourth Avenue for five minutes. When the flock took off again, about a hundred of the group lay dead on the street from starvation and exhaustion. The birds would end up having a better day than the rest of the country.

(LIGHTS UP ON THE NEW YORK STOCK EXCHANGE/PHONE BANK)

(We hear the din of the stock exchange about to begin its trading day. A man is on a wall phone.)

PHILO. Here's how it works. This man is a firm clerk. It's one minute before trading begins and he's on the phone with a broker at his firm. A customer wants to sell all 500 shares of his stock in Montgomery Ward. The firm clerk takes the order and passes it to one of the firm's floor traders.

(We're watching all this happen.)

PHILO. It's been a very bad week for the New York Stock Exchange as the Dow Jones has lost 10 percent of its value in just four days. There are strict rules on the trading floor: No running, pushing, cursing and suit coats must be worn at all times. 20 minutes from now those rules will go out the window, but right now it's 30 seconds before the start of trading and our floor trader has made it over to the section of the 16,000 square foot floor where retail stocks are being traded and goes to the Montgomery Ward post.

(We start to hear the pulsing sound.)

PHILO. At the post is the specialist for Montgomery Ward. His job is to match sellers with buyers and establish the strike price, that's somewhere between the ask and the offer. 15 seconds till the market opens.

(And the pulsing starts to build.)

SARNOFF. This doesn't have anything to do with anything.

PHILO. Yes it does, sir.

SARNOFF. Phil –

PHILO. Excuse me, this is my turn.

SARNOFF. Go ahead, re-live the damn thing.

PHILO. Now in that phone call, the clerk asked the broker if he had a limit price and the broker said, "Sell it at market" which means get whatever you can for it and that's 'cause after the last four days there are a lot more sellers than buyers. Now when there are more sellers than buyers and the men are no longer required to wear suit coats, I don't need to tell you what happens next. Ready?

(Ding! Ding! Ding!)

TRADER. *(shouting)* Selling 500 shares of Montgomery Ward!

SALES REP. *(shouting)* I'm taking 82.

TRADER. *(shouting)* What the hell are you talkin' about?

SALES REP. *(shouting)* Bobby –

TRADER. *(shouting)* What are you *talkin'* about, you closed at 97!

SALES REP. *(shouting)* I've got 25 sell orders at 82.

TRADER. *(shouting)* Ah *fuck*, Tony, we opened 10 seconds ago!

PHILO. These guys are pretty tired from spending the past four days losing other people's money and now that floor trader's got a decision to make. He can go back to the phones, call the broker and tell him the market price on Montgomery Ward's a lot lower than they're thinking, but that'll cost him a few minutes and it could cost the customer a few thousand dollars. He was told to sell at the market. Nobody wants to be at the beginning of an avalanche, but better that than at the end of one.

SARNOFF. Phil –

PHILO. The Cossacks are comin' again, David.

TRADER. *(shouting)* Alright, selling 500 shares of Montgomery Ward at 82 dollars a share!

(And with this, the other **TRADERS** *around the pit, convinced that the price is only going in one direction, begin shouting –)*

TRADERS. *(top of their lungs)* Selling 2000 shares at 81!/Selling!/Get me 79! 79!/ 1500 shares at 78! I'll take 78!/ Gimme 77 and a half!

PHILO. The sales rep takes the order, puts it in a pneumatic tube system where it's sent to a repository at the center of the trading floor and a teletype operator marks the price on a ticker wire. For anyone who understands what they're looking at, it only takes a minute to realize that something's going terribly wrong.

(LIGHTS UP ON SARNOFF'S OFFICE)

(Where **SARNOFF** *has his team gathered at the ticker machine giving him their analysis.)*

ANALYST. It's the volume, it's the volume of the trades. 45,000 shares of Anaconda Copper? 50,000 Standard Oil? I'm looking at – I can't believe I'm adding this right –

PHILO. You are.

ANALYST. 630,000 shares traded in the first 26 transactions.

SARNOFF. Where did we open?

ANALYST. I'm –

SARNOFF. This morning, where did we open?

WACHTEL. One-oh-one.

SARNOFF. We closed at 118.

WACHTEL. Yeah.

SARNOFF. We dropped 17 points a share while we were sleeping?!

ANALYST. They're called air pockets.

SARNOFF. *(shouting)* Betty!

ANALYST. You can fall 15, 20, 25 points at a time before you find a buyer.

SARNOFF. Air pockets.

PHILO. Light the torches.

SARNOFF. Shut your mouth.

(**BETTY** *steps in*)

BETTY. Yes sir.

SARNOFF. Get me the Chairman of the Federal Reserve.

(*LIGHTS UP ON CONFERENCE ROOM*)

PHILO. The Fed was already in an impromptu emergency session.

CHAIRMAN. The discussion will be do we lower the discount rate from six to five.

ADVISOR. We have to, sir. People are gonna require liquidity to meet what are going to be devastating margin calls.

CHAIRMAN. If we intervene and the market continues to dive then the Fed's gonna seem impotent.

MAN #1. We don't give a shit, Roy, this isn't an academic exercise. Confidence is being destroyed and fortunes are being lost.

CHAIRMAN. Holy Jesus God, Don, is the market crashing?

MAN #1 (DON). Mr. Chairman, we ain't seen nothin' yet.

(*LIGHTS CHANGE TO TRADING FLOOR*)

PHILO. By noon, the floor was four inches thick with paper. Everywhere you turned, the names that built the 20th Century were falling down around you. Union Carbide, Blue Ridge, Dow Chemical, ITT, US Steel. "Selling!," "Selling!" –

TRADERS. *(all together) Selling!*

PHILO. And as if things couldn't get worse –

(The sound of the din and the pulse grows louder.)

TRADER. *(shouting on the phone)* The ticker is 88 minutes behind!

PHILO. – the typists couldn't keep up with the orders.

TRADER. *(louder into the phone)* I said the ticker is 88 minutes behind! Clients are giving us sell orders based on what the market price was an *hour and a half ago!* The bankers are gonna have to step up and roll back the margins. Guys are gettin' killed out here!

(LIGHTS UP ON BANKER MEETING)

PHILO. The heads of National City Bank, Chase National Bank, Bankers Trust and Guaranty Trust gathered at New York's biggest investment bank, the House of Morgan.

BANKER #1. If we go and buy –

BANKER #2. Thomas –

BANKER #1 (THOMAS). If we buy –

BANKER #2. Listen to me –

BANKER #1. If we go in now and buy like crazy it'll prop up confidence, it'll prop up prices.

BANKER #2. Which is what Charley Mitchell said last Thursday when he went in for U.S. Steel and got hit in the head with a hundred tons of sheet metal.

BANKER #3. What about the calls?

(silence)

Gentlemen, what about the margin calls?

BANKER #2. Some people are going to get hurt.

PHILO. When you buy on margin, you're essentially taking out a loan. And if the stock price becomes "impaired" – falls below a certain point – the bank can call in the loan. So every broker in NY is trying to call every client in the country to tell them that not only is their investment gone but they actually *owe* money to a bank.

BROKER. *(into phone)* It's a margin call, Louis. You owe your account $8,000.

(silence)

Louis, do you understand? There's nothing left and you owe the bank $8000.

LOUIS. *(pause)* I don't under – how do they expect me to –

PHILO. They're gonna take your house.

(Clang! Clang! Clang! Clang! Clang!)

PHILO. See how I ended that, David? With the metaphor of the house?

SARNOFF. It was exquisitely subtle, Phil, you done?

PHILO. No, we gotta check the scoreboard. 24 hours earlier RCA was worth a hundred and eighteen dollars a share. What are you worth now?

(SARNOFF is sifting through the ticker tape while a few EXECUTIVES stand by. The pulsing continues, though it got much slower and deliberate when trading was rung to a close above.)

WACHTEL. *(beat)* David?

(SARNOFF's looking...looking...looking...)

SARNOFF. 42.

(The pulsing sound ends.)

PHILO. He'd predicted a price adjustment but nothing like that. He was also right about the Federal Courts busting the patent pool as an illegal monopoly. He was gonna have to make some concessions in the settlement, one of which was that there'd be no more horseshit rules about advertising over the airwaves. It's every station owner for himself and you got a problem with that you can drag someone else's ass to the woodshed 'cause your stock's at 42 and you're done.

SARNOFF. That's not what happened.

PHILO. You needed to pull a rabbit out of a hat.

SARNOFF. That's not what happened.

PHILO. What am I getting wrong?

SARNOFF. I was *already* giving Zworykin two-hundred thousand a year for research, I was *already* giving him a staff the size of –

PHILO. And he wasn't getting anywhere! And the market crashed right on your face and you had to let the station owners sell time on the news *and you'd had it!* Zworykin's not getting anywhere. Enough. Go to his lab.

SARNOFF. That's not why it happened.

PHILO. Why what happened? *(beat)* That's not why what happened, David?

SARNOFF. It's called opposition research.

PHILO. It's also called corporate espionage, isn't it?

SARNOFF. Pretty low-tech espionage, wouldn't you say?

PHILO. I would.

SARNOFF. Did he come in disguise? Phil? Did he come in disguise?

PHILO. No.

SARNOFF. Did he give you a false name?

PHILO. No.

SARNOFF. He told you his name.

PHILO. I knew his name.

SARNOFF. Did he break into your lab?

PHILO. I think we've been through this enough.

SARNOFF. How did he get into your lab?

PHILO. I invited him.

SARNOFF. And up in the lab –

PHILO. I'm not a professional witness anymore, I don't –

SARNOFF. – did he hit you over the head, did he drug you, did he do something while your back was turned?

PHILO. No.

SARNOFF. Don't casually accuse me of theft.

PHILO. I'm gonna accuse you of whatever I want, but if you think I'm doing it casually you're out of your mind. You *sent* him to my lab.

SARNOFF. It wasn't like it was a secure area.

PHILO. Scientists aren't supposed to operate in secret, you share as much information as you can.

SARNOFF. You were *eager* to show it to him.

PHILO. I had a light problem.

SARNOFF. No, you had a huge light problem. If you hadn't, it would've been done by now. If you hadn't, you would've owned television. If you hadn't –

(practically through gritted teeth, turning into a shout)

– somebody, somewhere – anybody – anywhere – *anyone other than me – would have heard of you!*

PHILO. I really ended up in your nightmares, didn't I.

SARNOFF. I sleep fine.

PHILO. How did he know where I was?

SARNOFF. *(beat)* What?

PHILO. How did he know where –

SARNOFF. Your lab was at 202 Green Street, he told the cab driver "Take me to 202 – "

PHILO. I wasn't at the lab when we met. How'd he know where I'd be?

SARNOFF. *(to the audience)* Because he'd become a fairly famous guy in San Francisco. All the papers carried the story when he got that first picture but it was almost two years later and he still couldn't get an image that was worth anything without focusing an impractical amount of light on the object. He was understandably obsessed with finding an answer and had taken to sleeping just two or three hours a night on a cot in the storage room. He had a son now, Kenny, who was 20-months-old and every night around midnight when the others would go home to catch some sleep, he'd build Kenny a toy in the lab. One night he built him a sundial that would tell time on the moon. *(beat)* Told him he'd be able to use it one day.

(LIGHTS UP ON PHILO'S LAB)

(EVERSON, GORRELL, STAN, HARLAN and AGNES are waiting.)

SARNOFF. Crocker, Everson and Gorrell had lost faith and money and were looking to sell The Farnsworth Television Company and on this morning, Philo was supposed to demonstrate television to the owners of United Artists. Everson and Gorrell were desperate to make a good impression. It wasn't gonna happen.

(SCHENCK, FAIRBANKS and PICKFORD are led in by CLIFF.)

EVERSON. Good morning, I'm George Everson.

SCHENCK. Joseph Schenck.

PICKFORD. It's nice to meet you, I'm Mary Pickford, and this is Doug.

EVERSON. Of course, it's a pleasure. Leslie Gorrell.

GORRELL. Good morning.

SCHENCK. Please thank Bill Crocker for arranging this.

EVERSON. No it's our pleasure. Philo should be here at any moment. *(beat)* You met Cliff. And this is Mr. Farnsworth's sister, Agnes.

AGNES. Hello.

PICKFORD. How do you do.

FAIRBANKS. Nice to meet you.

AGNES. He should be out in just a moment.

SCHENCK. We're very excited.

(There's an awkward silence… hen…)

EVERSON. This is Stan Willis.

STAN. Hello.

PICKFORD. Hello.

FAIRBANKS. Hello.

EVERSON. And Harlan Honn.

HARLAN. Hello.

FAIRBANKS. Good to see you.

PICKFORD. Hi.

EVERSON. *(pause)* Harlan's been doing some incredible things with refrigeration?

GORRELL. They don't care.

EVERSON. I thought while they were waiting they might like to hear about –

GORRELL. Freon? No. Agnes? Would you go back and get your brother.

AGNES. Yeah. I'm sure he's making some last minute tube adjustments. *(pause)* That's adjustments to the tube.

GORRELL. We got that, Agnes. Could you please?

(*LIGHTS CHANGE TO STORAGE ROOM*)

(*A small room with a cot. A bottle of Bushmills and a glass sits nearby.*)

AGNES. Phil. *(pause)* Phil!

(*And the cot pops up.* PHILO's *been sleeping under it.*)

PHILO. *(simply used to it.)* Ow.

AGNES. *(picking up the bottle and stowing it)* They're here.

PHILO. Who?

AGNES. The people.

PHILO. Now?

AGNES. Yes, they're in the lab. Straighten yourself up.

PHILO. When are they getting here?

AGNES. They're here.

PHILO. Right. You just said that.

AGNES. You're drunk.

PHILO. No. Yes, yes, I am.

AGNES. God –

PHILO. We've gotta make it a fast one today, we have a – what's the woman's name again?

AGNES. Mary Pickford.

PHILO. Pickford, got it.

AGNES. Yes, she's the most famous woman in the world so there's really no reason you would have heard of her.

PHILO. I didn't say I hadn't heard of her, I just didn't know it was her that was coming *today.*

AGNES. Why were you *under* the cot?

PHILO. I don't know but that's not an unreasonable question. Pickford?

AGNES. Yes.

(LIGHTS CHANGE BACK TO LAB)

(As **PHILO** *and* **AGNES** *come in.)*

PHILO. Good morning, everyone, I'm sorry, I'm Philo Farnsworth.

EVERSON. Phil, this is Joe Schenck.

PHILO. Nice to meet you. This is the lab gang.

*(***PEM***'s come in from the front.)*

PEM. Excuse me.

PHILO. And that is my wife, Pem.

PEM. Nice to meet you.

SCHENCK. Likewise.

PHILO. Pem, this is Mary Pickford.

PEM. I'm a great admirer.

PICKFORD. Aren't you sweet.

PHILO. And of course, a man who needs no introduction, Mr. Charlie Chaplin.

FAIRBANKS. *(beat)* Were you talking about me?

PHILO. Yes.

FAIRBANKS. I'm Doug Fairbanks.

AGNES. Philo!

PHILO. *Dammit.*

PEM. *(to* **FAIRBANKS***)* Of course you are and you're wonderful.

PHILO. I apologize, Mr. Chaplin. Mr. *Fairbanks.*

GORRELL. I've stepped off the edge of the world.

FAIRBANKS. Chaplin's shorter and considerably more talented.

PICKFORD. Charlie did want to be here today but he's on a scoring stage.

EVERSON. Why don't we start the demonstration.

GORRELL. Yes, for the love of everything holy.

PHILO. Sure.

PEM. I'm sorry. Phil?

GORRELL. Now?

PEM. Yes.

PHILO. Excuse me.

(*LIGHTS CHANGE TO CORRIDOR*)

(*As* **PHILO** *and* **PEM** *step in.*)

PEM. Kenny's still got the cough.

PHILO. All night?

PEM. Yeah.

PHILO. Where is he now?

PEM. Mrs. Palmer's sitting with him. I want to take him to the doctor Bill recommended.

PHILO. Sure, absolutely.

PEM. It's gonna cost $10 just for the visit.

PHILO. Well then that's what it costs.

PEM. Okay. Go back to work.

PHILO. Okay.

(*LIGHTS UP ON LAB*)

(*As* **PHILO** *steps back in.*)

PHILO. Okay. When light hits Mary Pickford it gets excited. The *photons* – light is made up of *photons* – the *photons* get excited, which means they move. Now, once they move, they can be manipulated by photoelectric material and captured in this tube. And then they can be sent by an electronic transmitter to a cathode. A cathode makes *photons* glow. So what have we done – well, we've re-constructed a light image of Mary Pickford, formed by the *photons* she excited. And though the effect is almost instantaneous, it's done line by horizontal line.

FAIRBANKS. Extraordinary.

PHILO. Wouldn't you think so, Charlie?

FAIRBANKS. Doug.

PHILO. But here's the problem.

FAIRBANKS. What.

PHILO. It doesn't work.

> (**GORRELL** *lets his head bang against the nearest hard surface.*)

GORRELL. *(head down)* It works. He's kidding. He has a play-ful sense of humor.

PHILO. Yeah it works, you're gonna see it work, but it doesn't work well. The amount of light needed to get a picture that any of you would be interested in would blind you. You know why? *(pause)* No, I'm really asking, does anyone know why? We're going out of our *minds* in here!

(LIGHTS CHANGE TO CROCKER'S OFFICE)

CROCKER. It doesn't work?

PHILO. Bill –

CROCKER. You told the owners of United Artists that it doesn't work?

PHILO. Not all the owners, Chaplin was on a scoring stage.

CROCKER. It doesn't work?

PHILO. I said it didn't work very *well.*

CROCKER. Oh, much better.

PHILO. Bill, United Artists wasn't buying, neither was Philco, neither was Magnavox.

CROCKER. How do you know U.A. wasn't buying?

PHILO. Because it doesn't work very well.

GORRELL. I think your presentation could've been sunnier.

PHILO. *You* think *I* could be sunnier?

GORRELL. I do.

PHILO. I shouldn't be showing it yet, it's not ready. It's em-barrassing to me.

GORRELL. How do you mix up Charlie Chaplin with Errol Flynn?

PHILO. I mixed him up with Douglas Fairbanks but I think that's the least of our concerns.

CROCKER. What should be the most of our concerns?

PHILO. I always thought it was Gorrell.

CROCKER. Do I look like I'm in the mood for this?

PHILO. *(pause – seriously)* I have light falling on the cesium oxide coating and I charge it up with electrons. I move the charged image along an electrode, an aperture. And that's where the light dissipates. Bill, it is impossible that this problem can't be solved. It's something small and it's right under our noses.

GORRELL. How many times have you built and torn apart the image dissector?

PHILO. I don't know, I'd have to check the journals.

SARNOFF. Guess.

PHILO. Two-thousand times.

GORRELL. Jesus.

PHILO. *(to CROCKER)* It's right under our noses.

CROCKER. *(to EVERSON and GORRELL)* Lemme talk to Phil for a minute.

(EVERSON and GORRELL start to leave.)

EVERSON. *(to PHILO helpfully)* Chaplin is the Little Tramp, Fairbanks is the swashbuckler.

PHILO. I don't think they walk around town like that, but thanks, George.

(EVERSON exits.)

CROCKER. One in four adult American males are unemployed.

PHILO. I know.

CROCKER. 25 percent.

PHILO. Am I about to be one of them?

CROCKER. The economy's not turning around is my point.

PHILO. It will.

CROCKER. Do you know when?

PHILO. No.

CROCKER. Do you know when you'll have a picture suitable for commercial use?

PHILO. No.

CROCKER. Those two answers work terribly together.

PHILO. Before this century is over, a man is gonna walk on the moon, I swear to *God* that's gonna happen. And everyone in the world is gonna watch him do it on television.

CROCKER. I know. *(pause)* We're sure it's just engineering?

PHILO. Absolutely sure.

CROCKER. *(beat)* You'll try to make your presentations a little more optimistic?

PHILO. Yes sir.

CROCKER. All right.

(**PHILO** *starts to leave, then turns back –)*

PHILO. *(pause)* Bill, you know, I always meant to tell you I know you took a beating in the market, and I've always meant to tell you that I really admired the way you hung in there with Boeing, you didn't sell. It was a real act of...I don't know, it was a real act of patriotism I think. You could've –

CROCKER. I didn't. Hang in there. I was quiet about it that day, but I sold Boeing.

PHILO. *(beat)* Well that's okay too, you got a family.

CROCKER. No. My father's gonna come back from the grave and punch me in the head. My father and his brothers, you know they built the railroad. They wanted me to do what was next.

PHILO. You are. Don't sell your shares of The Farnsworth Television Company. I'm not gonna make fool outa you.

CROCKER. Well that ship sailed a long time ago but I appreciate it. Go home and get some sleep.

PHILO. I'm gonna meet my guys at the place and go back up to the lab.

SARNOFF. The sale or consumption of alcohol was against the law that year – a law that never produced fewer drinkers, just more criminals. How did I know where he'd be? 'cause I knew where he drank.

(LIGHTS CHANGE TO SPEAKEASY)

(CLIFF, STAN and HARLAN are entertaining three YOUNG WOMEN, whose faces we don't get to see yet.)

SARNOFF. There was a chess club on Green Street where for a nickel you could sit down and play chess or backgammon and have a cup of coffee or a cream soda. If they you knew you you could go in back.

CLIFF. *(seeing him)* Phil!

(HARLAN's in the middle of a story with the THREE WOMEN so PHILO motions for CLIFF and STAN to come join him.)

STAN. Everything go all right over there?

PHILO. Yeah.

STAN. Crocker's not mad?

PHILO. No, he's mad, but –

CLIFF. We're all right?

PHILO. Yeah. Where did you meet the women?

STAN. They're secretaries from back east. They're on vacation in San Francisco and they got in here somehow. You know, Phil, seriously, working in television has made it easier to meet girls.

PHILO. *(beat)* Well then it's all been worth it, Stan.

CLIFF. And that man at the bar has been asking when you'll be in.

PHILO. Who is he?

CLIFF. I don't know, he's Russian.

PHILO. You guys get the secretaries, I get the Russian guy at the bar?

STAN. That's the only reason Pem lets us live.

(PHILO nods that he can identify with that as he heads to the bar and stands a few feet from ZWORYKIN, who's nursing a drink.)

BARTENDER. Bushmills rocks?

PHILO. Thanks.

(The **BARTENDER** *starts making the drink.)*

PHILO. You know, Leslie Gorrell says I'm drinking too much. So does Pem.

BARTENDER. Nah. I'll let you know.

PHILO. *(to* **ZWORYKIN***)* Excuse me. You were asking after me. I'm Philo Farnsworth.

ZWORYKIN. Relative to what?

PHILO. I'm sorry?

ZWORYKIN. They say you're drinking too much relative to what?

*(***PHILO** *smiles and stares at the man for a moment...)*

PHILO. You're Vladimir Zworykin.

ZWORYKIN. Yes. And I've come to meet you.

PHILO. Maybe my wife's right, maybe God did walk in Utah.

ZWORYKIN. Is that what she thinks?

PHILO. I meant that you couldn't have come at a better time. I'm really happy to meet you. My whole lab follows your work real closely.

ZWORYKIN. What I would like, I would like to have a drink with you. Then we go across the street and you show me your image dissector. This device that breaks light down line by line...the way we plow a field. *(beat)* I follow you closely too.

PHILO. *(smiles)* We're gonna do better than that.

(calling)

Fellas.

(then to **ZWORYKIN***)*

We're gonna have a drink, go across the street, and then build one right in front of you.

(to **CLIFF, STAN** *and* **HARLAN***)*

Guys, come meet Vladimir Zworykin.

(LIGHTS CHANGE TO LAB)

SARNOFF. To his credit, Zworykin didn't want to go to San Francisco. He was a proud man who'd been working on television his whole life and always felt like he was one small step away. Up in the lab they opened another bottle and began building an image dissector.

(They're sitting and standing around the table. **PHILO** *working and the others handing him instruments at the precise moment he needs them. They might show a particular piece to Zworykin before it gets soldered on.)*

ZWORYKIN. I was in Berlin when the war broke out in 1914 after leaving the lab of –

STAN. Paul Langevin.

ZWORYKIN. Yes. In Paris. I went back to St. Petersburg, which is now Leningrad, and was – what's the word when you're taken into the army –

PHILO & STAN. Conscripted.

ZWORYKIN. I was conscripted. I was a lieutenant assigned to the Russian Wireless Telegraph and Telephone Company and I made a close study of the latest in vacuum tubes. I also made a close study of a young dental student named Tatiana Vasilieff.

STAN. Your wife.

ZWORYKIN. Correct.

HARLAN. Now, this rod'll be hot, Mr. Zworykin, you don't want to –

ZWORYKIN. I know exactly how hot it is.

HARLAN. Yes sir.

ZWORYKIN. I was certain after my success with Rosing, with Langevin and with the vacuum tubes, I would develop a method by which we could see from a distance. Then I found out the police were looking for me.

STAN. Why?

ZWORYKIN. They were having a revolution.

STAN. Ah.

ZWORYKIN. Yeah. *(beat)* The things I coulda done? The fucking things I coulda done.

(CLIFF enters with a glass tube.)

CLIFF. Here it is.

PHILO. Cliff's tube'll have to cool for a couple of hours but let me show you what it looks like when it does.

ZWORYKIN. Tatiana went to Germany, I went to Pittsburgh.

(**PHILO** *grabs a cathode tube and hands it to* **ZWORY-KIN.**)

STAN. Pittsburgh's all right, I've been to Pittsburgh.

(*to* **HARLAN**)

The confluence of which three rivers?

HARLAN. The Monongahela, the Allegheny –

ZWORYKIN. (*handling the tube*) I don't understand.

HARLAN. – and either the Missouri or Mississippi...

ZWORYKIN. I don't understand.

PHILO. You see something we did wrong?

ZWORYKIN. No. The seal on the tube. The Pyrex seal. You've sealed an optically clear disk of Pyrex onto the end of the dissector tube.

PHILO. Cliff did. Yeah, that was our first breakthrough.

ZWORYKIN. I'd been assured, both by Westinghouse and GE, I'd been assured that this couldn't be done.

PHILO. Well don't feel bad, I'd been assured of the same thing by every glassblower in San Francisco.

ZWORYKIN. How'd you do it?

CLIFF. Me?

ZWORYKIN. Yes.

CLIFF. I didn't know any better.

(**AGNES** *hurries in.*)

AGNES. Phil –

PHILO. Aggie, what are you doing here so –

AGNES. Come with me quick, Phil. It's Kenny.

(*LIGHTS CHANGE TO HOSPITAL*)

(*Where* **PEM** *is standing with two* **DOCTORS** *as* **PHILO** *comes in.*)

PEM. These are the doctors. This is my husband.

DOCTOR #1. It's a streptococcal infection and we're concerned it might spread to his lungs. We want to perform a preventive tracheotomy and we want to do it right now.

PHILO. Well, you're not gonna cut my son's throat open so let's figure out something else.

DOCTOR #1. Sir –

PHILO. He's two years old, we're gonna figure out something else.

DOCTOR #2. There isn't anything else.

PHILO. Talk me through the problem.

DOCTOR #1. Mr. Farnsworth, we don't have time to teach you medicine.

PHILO. I'm a very quick study.

DOCTOR #2. Look –

PHILO. The infection, is it caused by a virus or is it caused by a bacteria.

DOCTOR #2. Bacteria.

PHILO. Can alcohol be injected selectively into cells?

DOCTOR #2. Why would you want to inject –

PHILO. It kills germs.

DOCTOR #1. No, it can't be injected selectively.

PHILO. Why not?

PEM. Phil –

PHILO. Why not?

DOCTOR #2. Can you imagine the size of the instrument I'd need to do that?

PHILO. Alright.

DOCTOR #2. Look, we need to clear the trachea and the only way to do that –

PHILO. No. Tissue is full of salt water, salt water conducts electricity. What if we put electro-magnets on the outside of his throat?

DOCTOR #1. Sir –

PHILO. Listen to me, a coil that wraps around his throat –

DOCTOR #2. Even if there were such a device –

PHILO. I can build one.

PEM. Phil.

PHILO. *(to* **PEM***)* It'll take me two hours, I can build one.

DOCTOR #1. *(pause)* Mr. Farnsworth, Dr. Westbrook needs to begin preparing your son for surgery. You'll need to stay out here.

PHILO. I can build one!

DOCTOR #1. You'll need to stay out here.

(And the lights go to black as we hear a timpani roll and a speaker announce –)

ANNOUNCER. Ladies and gentlemen, welcome to the opening of the greatest auditorium on earth, the Radio City Music Hall.

(And we HEAR an orchestra begin as –)

(LIGHTS CHANGE TO RADIO CITY LOBBY)

(Where an **USHER** *is holding a telephone as* **SARNOFF** *comes out in a tuxedo.)*

USHER. Mr. Sarnoff?

SARNOFF. Yeah.

USHER. For you, sir.

SARNOFF. *(into phone)* This is David. *(listens)* Yeah. *(listens)* I'll be there to see it first thing in the morning.

(He gives the phone back as **LIZETTE** *comes out in an evening gown.)*

LIZETTE. David –

SARNOFF. That was Charlie, that was good news.

LIZETTE. What is it?

SARNOFF. Vladimir got a picture. A clear one using manageable light.

LIZETTE. Vladimir got a picture?

SARNOFF. A *good* picture with photographers lamps. Charlie says it's the clearest picture that's ever been transmitted.

LIZETTE. So now what happens?

SARNOFF. Well I'm gonna take the train down to Camden in the morning and see for myself.

LIZETTE. I don't understand.

SARNOFF. I'm gonna go to Camden in the morning.

LIZETTE. And then what?

SARNOFF. What do you mean?

LIZETTE. I don't understand.

SARNOFF. I'm taking a railroad train to Camden in the morning and looking at the picture.

LIZETTE. And then what do you do with it?

SARNOFF. I do what I do.

LIZETTE. *(to an USHER)* I'm Mrs. Sarnoff, could I have my coat please, I'm leaving.

SARNOFF. What the hell are you –

LIZETTE. I'm leaving.

(to the USHER)

I'll be waiting out front.

SARNOFF. Liz. Liz.

(LIZETTE exits.)

SARNOFF. *(to the USHERS)* It's a lot of fun being me.

(LIGHTS CHANGE TO STREET)

(As SARNOFF comes out.)

SARNOFF. You're gonna freeze out here.

LIZETTE. No I'm not.

SARNOFF. Well I'm gonna freeze out here.

LIZETTE. Tatiana Zworykin said Vladimir went to San Francisco last month.

SARNOFF. Let's go back inside.

LIZETTE. Did he visit Farnsworth's lab?

SARNOFF. I have no idea.

LIZETTE. You're full of shit, David!

USHER. Your coat, Mrs. Sarnoff.

LIZETTE. Thank you.

SARNOFF. Thank you.

(to **LIZETTE**)

If we have this conversation in private then there's less chance I'm gonna read a transcript of it in the papers tomorrow.

LIZETTE. How is it that for ten years Vladimir can't get a picture and then a month after he gets back from San Francisco, Charlie Strauss says he's got the clearest –

SARNOFF. I don't know.

LIZETTE. Where has Betsy been?

SARNOFF. Who the hell is Betsy?

LIZETTE. Your secretary.

SARNOFF. Betty.

LIZETTE. Where has she been?

SARNOFF. She's been on vacation.

LIZETTE. In San Francisco. For five weeks.

SARNOFF. Her mother lives in San Francisco, her mother is sick.

LIZETTE. What's the Get Around Farnsworth Department?

SARNOFF. *What's happened to you tonight?!*

LIZETTE. I've heard people talk about the Get Around Farnsworth Department. You're obsessed –

SARNOFF. Liz –

LIZETTE. – with this ridiculous thing which will at best be a toy for rich people.

SARNOFF. That's not what it's gonna be.

LIZETTE. That wasn't the point.

SARNOFF. That's not what it's gonna be and that *is* the point. It's gonna change everything. It's gonna end ignorance and misunderstanding. It's gonna end illiteracy. It's gonna end war.

LIZETTE. *How?!*

SARNOFF. By pointing a camera at it.

LIZETTE. You think if Germany knows we can see them they won't march across Europe?

SARNOFF. I think when *we* see them do it *we'll* stop them.

LIZETTE. I think you need a vacation.

SARNOFF. So you've brought me out here to the sidewalk?

LIZETTE. You think I'm being funny? You know what you've done.

SARNOFF. Zworykin applied for a patent four years before Farnsworth.

LIZETTE. His didn't work.

SARNOFF. U.S. patent law is very complicated.

LIZETTE. Is it?

SARNOFF. In '23, Zworykin made what are called generic claims which, with modifications – engineering – *now work.*

LIZETTE. How?

SARNOFF. *I don't know yet, I'm taking a train to Camden in the morning!*

LIZETTE. It works because he got something from Farnsworth, and that's what you sent him to do. You knew you weren't marrying a stupid woman. I think you just stole television.

(LIGHTS CHANGE TO CROCKER'S OFFICE)

*(**CROCKER, EVERSON, GORRELL** and someone new are waiting. The mood is tense as **PHILO** comes in.)*

PHILO. What happened, what's going on?

CROCKER. This is Donald Lippincott. He's your lawyer, I'll pay the bills.

LIPPINCOTT. Mr. Farnsworth, I want you to know that I got a degree in electrical engineering before attending Law School and becoming president of the Patent Law Association of San Francisco.

PHILO. *(pause)* What the hell is going on?

CROCKER. Vladimir Zworykin at the Westinghouse Lab transmitted an electronic image.

PHILO. I'm sure he did, we showed him how to.

CROCKER. You showed him how to?

PHILO. Yeah.

EVERSON. When?

PHILO. He was out here three months ago.

CROCKER. What are you telling us?

PHILO. *(pause)* Bill, he was out here. He came into the place, he wanted to see the lab. We built an image dissector for him. What are you saying?

CROCKER. He went back to Camden, New Jersey and reverse engineered it.

PHILO. He doesn't work in Camden, he works in Pittsburgh.

CROCKER. Westinghouse moved their labs to Camden when RCA bought Victor Talking Machines. Westinghouse isn't a sister company under GE anymore, it is part of RCA.

PHILO. What does any of that matter?

GORRELL. David Sarnoff bought Westinghouse so he'd own Zworykin's '23 patent, which now works.

PHILO. Zworykin didn't have to come to my lab to find out how to make an image dissector. A patent application's public. I have to say exactly what I'm gonna I'm do and how I'm gonna do it. It's an instruction manual, all he had to do was read it.

LIPPINCOTT. That's not all he had to do.

PHILO. What do you mean?

CROCKER. Apparently it's a very good picture and he's only using Klieg Lamps.

PHILO. *(pause)* Wait, are you saying he stole from us or are you saying he's got something we don't have?

CROCKER. It has to be both.

PHILO. *(pause)* I think you're being paranoid.

CROCKER. Phil –

PHILO. There's an international community of scientists which, at this level, shares –

LIPPINCOTT. Do you remember this newspaper story?

(**LIPPINCOTT**'s *holding up the Chronicle.*)

PHILO. That's when we got the first picture, yes.

LIPPINCOTT. Philo, you've been at war with David Sarnoff since the day this showed up in New York City. *(beat)* So what we're gonna do is this. We're gonna file a patent interference suit. We're gonna take depositions and submit briefs to a lay court and ask it to grant priority of invention.

PHILO. And what happens then?

LIPPINCOTT. A judge in Delaware is going to decide who invented television.

CROCKER. *(beat)* Can you think of anything offhand that he might have seen in the lab which wasn't in your original invention?

(**PHILO** *doesn't say anything but he knows the answer.*)

CROCKER. Anything with the cesium? Potassium? Anything with the transmitter?

PHILO. It was the Pyrex seal. He didn't know there was a way to seal the tube.

SARNOFF. Nobody lied and nobody broke the law.

PHILO. *(to* **SARNOFF***)* Who were the girls in the bar? The secretaries?

SARNOFF. Nobody broke the law, Phil.

(*LIGHTS CHANGE TO SPEAKEASY*)

STAN. *(calling)* Phil!

(**PHILO** *stands there and* **STAN** *comes over.*)

STAN. Phil, you've been standing in the doorway for two minutes.

PHILO. The secretaries are here again?

STAN. Yeah, but Harlan and I had a new idea we wanted to –

PHILO. Excuse me.

(**PHILO** *walks right over to the women, one of whom we can see now is* **BETTY**.)

HARLAN. Phil! Ladies, this is the boy genius, this is Philo Farnsworth.

BETTY. Nice to meet you.

PHILO. What's your name?

(There's something threatening in **PHILO***'s tone and* **BETTY** *immediately knows he knows.)*

HARLAN. *(pause)* This is Betty. And this is Helen and –

PHILO. Where do you work?

HARLAN. *(beat)* They're on vacation from New York, Phil. Betty's seeing after her mom, who –

PHILO. Where do you work?

HARLAN. *(not understanding)* They're secretaries.

PHILO. Where do you work?

HARLAN. What's goin' on?

BETTY. I'm secretary to the president of RCA.

PHILO. *(turning to* **SARNOFF***) Are you kidding me with this shit?!*

SARNOFF. You're imagining it.

PHILO. *They're sitting right here!*

HARLAN. Phil?

SARNOFF. They were there *once*, they never came back.

PHILO. You think I'm delusional?

SARNOFF. *Kenny died! They cut his throat open and he died! You were half outa your mind! (beat)* The girls were there *once*.

PHILO. *(to* **CLIFF, HARLAN** *and* **STAN***)* I need to talk to you guys.

HARLAN. I didn't know they were from RCA, should we ask 'em up to the lab?

PHILO. Let's not.

STAN. Why?

PHILO. Well for one thing I'm not sure anymore that they're really there, but that's beside the point.

CLIFF. What's goin' on, Phil?

PHILO. Vladimir Zworykin has taken Cliff's tube and combined it with something he's got to produce what's apparently a very clear picture using thousand watt light. He's claiming it's a modification of his '23 design and asking a judge to grant him the patent on television. So we're suing him.

HARLAN. *(pause)* What?

PHILO. Yeah, things have taken a turn, but you really gotta ask yourself.

CLIFF. What?

PHILO. How the hell did he fix it?

(LIGHTS CHANGE TO STEPS OUTSIDE CHURCH)

(We hear funereal organ music as **MOURNERS** *mill around on the street. A* **MAN** *is talking to* **SARNOFF.***)*

MAN. He was a business man.

SARNOFF. *(to the audience)* A memorial service was held at St. Patrick's Cathedral on Fifth Avenue for Thomas Edison.

MAN. He was a businessman and I'll tell you why.

SARNOFF. I don't need you to tell me why.

MAN. He saw the electrical lines were an eyesore. So he said to the city, I will form a company and you will pay us to put the lines underground. Consolidated Edison. You see how he got paid twice?

SARNOFF. Maybe you want to stop talking.

MAN. I'm sayin' –

SARNOFF. The widow is walking over here.

*(***MINA EDISON*** has made her way over.)*

MINA. David.

SARNOFF. Mina.

MINA. This is a wonderful turnout. Thank you.

SARNOFF. This is all for Tom.

MINA. There's someone I want you to meet.

SARNOFF. I wanted to let you know that the lights in Rockefeller Center will go dim for two minutes tonight.

MINA. That's very nice, David. Thank you.

> *(calling)*

> Pem!

> **(PEM** *has come over from the group of mourners. She and* **SARNOFF** *immediately know who the other is.)*

MINA. Pem, this is David Sarnoff. David, this is Pem Farnsworth, the wife of Tom's young friend in San Francisco.

SARNOFF. *(pause)* I'm pleased to meet you.

PEM. Yes.

MINA. I'm sorry, what time did you say the lights would –

SARNOFF. At 8 PM.

MINA. I should join the kids.

SARNOFF. Sure.

> **(MINA** *exits and* **SARNOFF** *and* **PEM** *are alone.)*

SARNOFF. *(pause)* I understand your son died recently.

PEM. Yes.

SARNOFF. I'm sorry. Was it sudden?

PEM. Yes.

SARNOFF. How is your husband holding up? Something like this –

PEM. I certainly hope you're not trying to make a point about his mental health.

SARNOFF. I wasn't.

PEM. He couldn't be here, he had to stay in San Francisco.

SARNOFF. For the depositions.

PEM. They seem to be asking him a lot of questions about the level of formal education he's had. I assume your lawyers are preparing to argue that someone from Indian Creek with a year at BYU wouldn't be able to –

SARNOFF. I'm sure the lawyers would prefer we didn't discuss this.

PEM. Can I ask you something before we go in?

SARNOFF. Yes.

PEM. The Ford Motor Company had a problem with people stealing their customer's cars right off the street and they held a contest in *Science and Invention* Magazine to see who could come up with the best solution. Philo wrote in that you could magnetize the starting mechanism near the steering column and if you magnetized a key in the exact same way, then only that key would start that car and he won the contest. My husband invented the ignition lock. Which may not sound like much except he was 12 years old at the time. What were you doing when you were 12, Mr. Sarnoff?

SARNOFF. Well that would've been two years after my parents and I were run out of our house by cossacks, Mrs. Farnsworth. So I was teaching myself how to speak English. *(pause)* I'm sorry about your little boy.

(LIGHTS CHANGE TO LIPPINCOTT'S OFFICE)

(LIPPINCOTT is reading to CLIFF, STAN and HARLAN. PHILO is detached, looking through piles of papers.)

LIPPINCOTT. Here's Herbert Hoover talking about television. Sarnoff got Jim Harbord to plant the piece in a newspaper.

(reading)

"This invention again emphasizes a new era in the approach to scientific discovery. It is the result of *organized, planned and definitely directed* scientific research, magnificently coordinated in a *cumulative group* of highly skilled scientists."

STAN. So we know he's not talking about us.

HARLAN. No.

LIPPINCOTT. *(reading)* "– a cumulative group of highly skilled scientists, loyally supported by a great corporation devoted to the advancement of the art. The intricate process of this invention" – bear in mind, he's never seen one – "The intricate process of this invention could" – are you ready – "*never have been developed under any conditions of isolated effort.*" This is for anyone who still thinks I'm paranoid, Philo, are you listening?

PHILO. Am I what? No, sorry, Herbert Hoover is devoted to the arts how?

(Lippincott's **SECRETARY** *steps in –)*

SECRETARY. Mr. Lippincott?

LIPPINCOTT. *(to* **PHILO***)* What are you doing?

PHILO. Somewhere in here, he has to have described something that he's doing differently. Cliff, you're looking at the aperture?

CLIFF. Yeah.

LIPPINCOTT. Phil, I need your head in *this.*

*(***LIPPINCOTT** *steps over to his* **SECRETARY***.)*

SECRETARY. There's a man here who says he knows Mr. Farnsworth and can help.

LIPPINCOTT. What's his name?

SECRETARY. Uh… Justin Tillman?

LIPPINCOTT. *(calling)* Phil, you know anyone named Tillman?

PHILO. No.

LIPPINCOTT. Lemme see what he wants.

*(***LIPPINCOTT** *exits.)*

STAN. The coating? There's something with the photoelectric coating? He's got magic photoelectric coating?

HARLAN. Is it possible it's effected by humidity or atmospheric pressure or barometric pressure?

STAN. You think we haven't gotten a clear picture because the weather hasn't been good enough?

HARLAN. You're right. Let's re-visit your theory that he has magic photoelectric material.

*(***LIPPINCOTT** *re-enters with* **JUSTIN TOLMAN***.)*

LIPPINCOTT. Phil?

TOLMAN. Philo, do you remember who I am?

*(***PHILO** *looks up…in his present state of mind this is almost like a mirage.)*

PHILO. Mr. Tolman?

LIPPINCOTT. So you do know each other?

TOLMAN. I taught Philo Basic Science in high school.

HARLAN. Wow. *(beat)* Who taught *you?*

PHILO. Mr. Tolman, what are you doing here?

TOLMAN. My wife and I moved here last year. I read about this in the local paper. I'm not sure if this'll mean anything, but I thought maybe you could use it.

(TOLMAN's taken out a science textbook. He opens to a certain page and takes out a folded piece of paper and unfolds it on the desk.)

TOLMAN. You drew this for me. First week of September, 1921.

HARLAN. Look at that.

STAN. Shit.

HARLAN. Look at that.

STAN. It's the image dissector.

CLIFF. There's the seal.

HARLAN. Yeah.

LIPPINCOTT. Did you say '21?

TOLMAN. Hm?

LIPPINCOTT. Did you say he drew this in 1921?

TOLMAN. First week of September.

LIPPINCOTT. Mr. Tolman, would you give a deposition in this matter?

TOLMAN. Yes sir.

STENOGRAPHER. Would you state your full name, please?

TOLMAN. Justin Tolman.

ACTOR #1. Charles Strauss.

ACTOR #2. Ernst Alexanderson.

(The stage has begun to fill with witnesses being deposed.)

WACHTEL. Edward Wachtel.

ACTOR #3. I have Bachelors and Masters degrees from the Massachusetts Institute of Technology in Mechanical Engineering –

ACTOR #4. A Ph.D in Electrical Engineering –

ACTOR #5. My Ph.D's in Chemistry –

ACTOR #2. – the faculty of the Rensselaer Polytechnic Institute –

ACTOR #6. – the Princeton Institute of Advanced Studies –

ACTOR #4. – at the United States Naval Academy at Annapolis, Maryland.

SARNOFF. And for the visiting team?

STAN. I left Cal Tech after my junior year to work for Mr. Farnsworth.

TOLMAN. I taught him high school science in Rigby, Idaho.

CLIFF. He's married to my sister.

STENOGRAPHER. Would you state your full name, please.

ZWORYKIN. Vladimir Kosma Zworykin. Z-W-O-R-Y-K-I-N

(LIGHTS CHANGE TO CONFERENCE ROOM)

*(***ZWORYKIN*** is being deposed. This is all routine and without courtroom theatrics. ***PHILO*** and ***LIPPINCOTT*** sit at the table. ***PHILO*** is still going through all the papers and diagrams.)*

LAWYER. Mr. Zworykin, did you make a patent application in 1923?

ZWORYKIN. Yes.

LAWYER. Would you describe your invention?

ZWORYKIN. The system disclosed by my application utilizes a cathode ray tube as the element for translating the optical image into the electrical wave train of...

SARNOFF. Now something incredible is about to happen and these lawyers are thoroughly unprepared for it.

ZWORYKIN. ...so as to reconstruct there an electro-optical representation of the impressed or in-falling optical image.

LAWYER. In the 11 years since that application have you made any modifications?

SARNOFF. Hang on.

ZWORYKIN. Yes.

LAWYER. Would you name one of those modifications?

PHILO. *(suddenly and right to* ZWORYKIN*)* You store the light.

SARNOFF. He just saw it.

LIPPINCOTT. Phil –

PHILO. You *store* the light.

LAWYER. Mr. Lippincott, your client can't –

PHILO. *(reading)* "In place of the usual fluorescent end wall –

LIPPINCOTT. Phil!

PHILO. – portion of the tube, Zworykin replaces this structure with a new type of composite or mosaic electrode –

LIPPINCOTT. You're speaking out loud!

PHILO. You stored the light!

ZWORYKIN. Yes!

SARNOFF. Vladimir jumps in.

LAWYER. Gentlemen –

ZWORYKIN. You were using *continuous* potassium coating –

LAWYER. Mr. Zworykin –

ZWORYKIN. I used droplets –

PHILO. I'm seeing that!

ZWORYKIN. – or globules, you see? The mosaic.

PHILO. And the different elemental areas stored the light.

ZWORYKIN. Yes.

LIPPINCOTT. *Gentlemen!*

PHILO. *(exhausted – breathing heavy)* You did it, you found it.

LIPPINCOTT. I'd like to take a five minute break now.

LAWYER. Yeah, me too.

SARNOFF. The lawyers were also unable to recognize signs of a nervous breakdown.

PHILO. Hey come on. Fellas. I mean whichever way this ends up going…I mean, it's done. It's done. We have television now.

(A JUDGE *enters and puts a heavy book down along with a pile of briefs and makes a few administrative notations during the following.)*

SARNOFF. There was no formality or gravity to the judge's decision. I don't even know if he was wearing a robe when he read it. It was one of three or four dozen pieces of business before the Court that morning, most of them having to do with a new design for a toaster.

JUDGE. You can sit, this'll just take a second. The Court's reviewed the briefs submitted by the parties and is ready to rule. The only question in controversy is whether the optical Pyrex seal at the end of the cathode tube constitutes new matter in Zworykin's 1923 application. I find that it does not and that it does in fact –

HARLAN. *You gotta be kidding me!*

CLIFF. Ah!

CROCKER. No!

JUDGE. Excuse me. *(beat)* And that it does in fact fall within generic claims made in that application. A decree will be entered awarding priority of invention to Vladimir Zworykin and authorizing the Commissioner of Patents to approve the original 1923 application. This matter is adjourned.

SARNOFF. I may be wrong, he may have won that first one and lost on appeal. Or lost and then won and lost again, I don't know, it went for a long time – the suits and counter-suits and appeals. It didn't matter, all I needed to do was run down the clock on his 17 years and that was easy 'cause by this time we were getting ready for war and everybody's resources were being directed toward developing an instrument based on the idea that targets reflect radio signals and create an echo. Radio Detection and Ranging, it was called, or radar for short. The lawyers and the investors and the friends had left, and then Farnsworth and Zworykin exchanged a few words before Zworykin slipped out the side door and Farnsworth and I were left alone.

(**PHILO** *has turned around and sees* **SARNOFF** *on the other side of the stage.*)

SARNOFF. I'm David Sarnoff.

PHILO. I'm Philo Farnsworth.

SARNOFF. Sure.

PHILO. You come all the way down from New York?

SARNOFF. Sure. *(beat)* What did you say to Zworykin?

PHILO. Hm?

SARNOFF. For posterity's sake. Did you tell him to fuck off?

PHILO. No. I asked him how he fell on the mosaic pattern for light storage.

SARNOFF. How did he do it?

PHILO. A lab assistant left a tube in an oven too long and the silver boiled up into little pieces. You should find out the name of that lab assistant and write it down somewhere. He and my brother-in-law built the first television.

SARNOFF. Listen, I'm sure your lawyer's told you that this decision has no legal effect on your patent, just ours.

PHILO. Is that right?

SARNOFF. No I mean it.

PHILO. You ever hear of Elisha Gray?

SARNOFF. No.

PHILO. He invented the telephone. And then showed up at the patent office exactly 120 minutes after Alexander Graham Bell.

SARNOFF. This isn't like that. You're free to license your patent and so are we.

PHILO. And in a side by side comparison between RCA and The Farnsworth Television Company, where do you suppose the manufacturers are gonna go? I just lost other people's money, I just lost television and I won't lie to you, Mr. Sarnoff, the billion dollars I'm not gonna get might have come in handy. So don't patronize me.

SARNOFF. How did your son die?

PHILO. What?

SARNOFF. I'm sorry, how did your son die?

PHILO. He died of strep throat.

SARNOFF. What are you gonna do now?

PHILO. I have to call my wife and apologize for wasting her time.

SARNOFF. Come work for RCA. We have a lab in Camden, a lab in Schenectady. You move your family there, you're put on salary.

PHILO. I appreciate it but no thank you.

SARNOFF. Why?

PHILO. I don't want to be told what to invent and once I invent it I don't want someone else owning it.

SARNOFF. So what are you gonna do?

PHILO. Well, people are starting to talk about fusion.

SARNOFF. I'm sorry?

PHILO. Fusion.

SARNOFF. What is it?

PHILO. What powers the rest of the universe. The sun gets its energy from hydrogen particles crashing into each other at hellacious speeds. Now, if we could re-create that in a controlled environment then theoretically all the energy you need to run the world you could find in this pen.

SARNOFF. Where are you gonna get the hydrogen?

PHILO. The whole place is made out of hydrogen.

SARNOFF. You're saying we're not gonna use petroleum?

PHILO. A gallon of water has 300 times as much energy as a gallon of gasoline. It doesn't cost anything and you're never gonna run out.

SARNOFF. You're crazy.

PHILO. I heard that a lot when I suggested we could transmit pictures electronically, which was 1921 by the way and there was no reason for your people to humiliate Justin Tolman like that.

SARNOFF. He was an old man with a crumpled piece of paper who'd forgotten a lot of things, including his home address. You sued *me*.

PHILO. Why did Edwin Armstrong kill himself?

SARNOFF. Don't believe everything you hear.

PHILO. The guy comes up with frequency modulation, then jumps off the top of a radio tower.

SARNOFF. The same thing killed Armstrong as killed you.

PHILO. You?

SARNOFF. No, but that's a good guess. Alcoholism.

PHILO. Maybe.

SARNOFF. Maybe?

PHILO. I know for sure that vomiting-on-my-shoes drunk I'm a better engineer than anyone you've got sober.

SARNOFF. Like I don't know that. Listen, you're not pissed off at me, you're pissed off 'cause no one in your lab left a tube in the oven too long. You never got it right.

PHILO. It was a hard problem.

SARNOFF. How hard?

PHILO. Zworykin never got it at *all* and if it weren't for me he'd still be spinning a pin wheel right now.

SARNOFF. Zworykin's a hack, he's second string, he's your understudy. You gave it away.

PHILO. You're talking to *me* about giving it away?

SARNOFF. If you'd a been smart – or sober –

PHILO. *(imitating* **SARNOFF***)* "...the opportunity to lift ourselves intellectually, culturally, spiritually, economically."

SARNOFF. You're a fan of my speeches.

PHILO. *(imitating)* "Radio should be run like a public library. Like a library." Whatever happened to no paid advertising during informational programming? You're talking to *me* about giving it away?

SARNOFF. I didn't have a choice.

PHILO. You're the president of RCA and the founder of the National Broadcasting Company, you had a variety of choices.

SARNOFF. No I didn't.

PHILO. We both blew it huge, but the difference is, I didn't *know* the answer to my light dissipation problem. You *knew* that once there was a financial incentive for a news broadcast to be popular it would be making a mockery out of both of our lives, to say nothing of a society being informed enough to participate in its own democracy.

SARNOFF. Yes.

PHILO. Yes?

SARNOFF. I made one single miscalculation in my life and that was that I had no idea how successful the thing was gonna be at delivering consumers to advertisers. And my friend, once you're good at that you're gonna have a hard time being good at anything else.

PHILO. Really?

SARNOFF. Yeah.

PHILO. How hard? *(silence)* You said 'go fuck yourself' to a Russian soldier when you were 10 but you couldn't say no to advertising dollars? You tried really hard but you couldn't?

SARNOFF. God, Phil, that wouldn't have been your way of calling me a kike by any chance, would it?

PHILO. David, I don't give a shit if you think Jesus Christ is the Messiah or not. I'm married to a woman who'll believe in Santa Claus before she'll believe Darwin.

SARNOFF. If you had it to do over, would you have cashed out early and sold me the patent?

PHILO. If I had it to do over I'd discover an antibiotic for strep throat.

SARNOFF. *(pause)* Come work for RCA.

PHILO. Did you come down here to offer me a job?

SARNOFF. No. *(beat)* No I didn't, I came down here to tell you that I think your invention is extraordinary. I wanted to tell you that and to say that it's my intention to be a worthy custodian.

PHILO. *(pause)* Good luck.

(**PHILO** *extends his hand.* **SARNOFF** *shakes it. Then* **PHILO** *exits.*)

SARNOFF. I never met Philo Farnsworth, I just made that last scene up. I wish I'd – I should've met with him, I couldn't. I'd attract attention so if I'd met with him – or if I'd offered him a job – it doesn't matter. By and large that was the last anyone heard from him. He was hospitalized in 1949 for depression. He'd live another 25 years after that, but he died drunk and broke and in obscurity.

(pause)

Pete Conrad was the third man on the moon. And when he stepped off the LEM, he radioed back what you'd expect, the usual... "Houston, Tranquility Base. Such and such is operational" and so on and then he stops. And he looks around and he feels what's under his feet and in an entirely different voice says, "My God. We were meant to be explorers."

(beat)

Then a moment later he said, "And good luck, Mr. Fitzhugh." I got a chance to meet Conrad later and I asked him what did you mean when you said, "Good luck, Mr. Fitzhugh"? Apparently the Fitzhughs were his neighbors growing up and one night he heard them fighting and Mrs. Fitzhugh shouted, "Oral sex?! You'll get oral sex when that kid next door walks on the moon!"

(beat)

I don't understand people who say what business do we have going to the moon when people around the world are starving. First of all, people aren't starving because we went to the moon, one doesn't have much to do with the other. But you go to the moon 'cause it's next. We came out of the cave, went over the hill, crossed the ocean, pioneered a continent and took to the heavens. We were meant to be explorers. Explorers, builders and protectors. I don't think I stole television – if I did,

I did it fair and square. But he deserved better in my hands. He was gonna do a lot more, but I burned his house down so he wouldn't burn mine down first.

(beat)

That's all, except for this. Every once in a while I have a very romantic vision.

(LIGHTS COME ON A BAR)

(The place is full and everyone is facing downstage, watching a television that's mounted up in the corner but which we can't see. We hear the commentary.)

VOICE OVER. *We've passed the 60 second mark, power transfer is complete.*

SARNOFF. It's July 16, 1969, at 9:30 am. A bar is filled with the kinds of people who are in bars at 9:30 am.

VOICE OVER. *We're on internal power with the launch vehicle at this time.*

SARNOFF. And down at the end of the bar is a guy with a Bushmills on the rocks. In front of him are a half-dozen cocktail napkins with ungodly diagrams scrawled all over them.

VOICE OVER. *All the second stage tanks now are pressurized. 30 seconds and counting, we are still go with Apollo 11.*

SARNOFF. No one in the bar would be able to recognize it, but what he's drawn is a diagram of a controlled hydrogen generator. Fusion.

VOICE OVER. *T-minus 25 seconds.*

BAR PATRON. Here they go.

VOICE OVER. *T-minus 20 seconds and counting.*

SARNOFF. And he hasn't lost his spirit, I haven't killed him. And he looks up at the television and he says –

PHILO. Godspeed fellas.

VOICE OVER. *T-minus 15 seconds, guidance is internal.*

SARNOFF. Godspeed.

VOICE OVER. *We have liftoff in 12, 11, 10, 9 – ignition sequence starts – 6, 5, 4, 3 –*

BLACKOUT

Also by
Aaron Sorkin...

A Few Good Men

Hidden In This Picture

Making Movies

Please visit our website **samuelfrench.com** for complete
descriptions and licensing information

OTHER TITLES AVAILABLE FROM SAMUEL FRENCH

ADRIFT IN MACAO
Book and Lyrics by Christopher Durang
Music by Peter Melnick

Full Length / Musical / 4m, 3f / Unit Sets
Set in 1952 in Macao, China, *Adrift In Macao* is a loving parody
of film noir movies. Everyone that comes to Macao is waiting
for something, and though none of them know exactly what
that is, they hang around to find out. The characters include
your film noir standards, like Laureena, the curvacious
blonde, who luckily bumps into Rick Shaw, the cynical surf-
and-turf casino owner her first night in town. She ends up
getting a job singing in his night club – perhaps for no reason
other than the fact that she looks great in a slinky dress. And
don't forget about Mitch, the American who has just been
framed for murder by the mysterious villain McGuffin. With
songs and quips, puns and farcical shenanigans, this musical
parody is bound to please audiences of all ages.